PUFFIN BOOKS

Warpath 6
Beach Assault

'Where's everyone else?' I shouted.

A man with a panzerfaust, the German equivalent of the bazooka, darted out of a doorway ahead of us. He took hasty aim, fired, and disappeared quickly. The bomb exploded against the starboard air intake. It did not penetrate the main armour, but the blast caused the engine to cut out. It took a full minute for me to restart it and still no other AVREs had arrived.

'Without support we've got no chance,' Gloomy yelled above the noise.

In that second, a horrible, icy thought shot through my mind – this is where you're going to die!

Read and collect the other books in the
Warpath *series*

WARPATH 6
Beach Assault

R. ELDWORTH

A fictional story
based on real-life events

PUFFIN BOOKS

PUFFIN BOOKS

Published by the Penguin Group
Penguin Books Ltd, 27 Wrights Lane, London W8 5TZ, England
Penguin Putnam Inc., 375 Hudson Street, New York, New York 10014, USA
Penguin Books Australia Ltd, Ringwood, Victoria, Australia
Penguin Books Canada Ltd, 10 Alcorn Avenue, Toronto, Ontario, Canada M4V 3B2
Penguin Books (NZ) Ltd, Private Bag 102902, NSMC, Auckland, New Zealand

On the World Wide Web at: www.penguin.com

Penguin Books Ltd, Registered Offices: Harmondsworth, Middlesex, England

First published 2000
1 3 5 7 9 10 8 6 4 2

Set in 11½/15pt Bookman Old Style

Made and printed in England by Clays Ltd, St Ives plc

British Library Cataloguing in Publication Data
A CIP catalogue record for this book is available from the British Library

ISBN 0-141-30721-8

R. Eldworth is a writer's name for Bryan Perrett. Bryan is a military historian who has
written many books. This is his second title for Puffin.

Contents

D-Day

The heavy casualties sustained during the Dieppe raid of 19 August 1942 convinced the Allies that when they came to mount a full-scale invasion of France it would be impossible to secure a French port. They decided, therefore, to invade over the open beaches of Normandy and bring their own prefabricated harbour with them. An elaborate deception plan was mounted to convince the enemy that the invasion would take place in the area of the Pas-de-Calais, which offered the shortest sea crossing from England. This was such a success that Hitler insisted on keeping his armoured divisions in that area. As a result, on 6 June 1944, when the real invasion took place in Normandy, the German Army was unable to mount an effective counter-attack.

Nevertheless, the Normandy coastline presented the Allies with many serious problems. Always formidable, the coastal defences had been considerably strengthened since the Dieppe raid. Tens of thousands of slave workers had used millions of tons of concrete to create bunkers that covered every inch of the landing beaches with the fire of their guns. There were also minefields, underwater obstacles, barbed-wire entanglements and anti-tank ditches. The defences were so strong that Hitler called them his Atlantic Wall.

In the British Army it was recognized that the key to the various problems involved in assaulting such positions lay in the use of specially designed armoured vehicles. In April 1943 Major-General P. C. S. Hobart, commander of the 79th Armoured Division, was informed that the Army's specialist tank and assault engineer units would be concentrated under his command, with the objective of developing the techniques and equipment that would be used to spearhead the coming invasion. Because of the strange collection of armoured vehicles it produced, the 79th Armoured Division became known as 'Hobo's Funnies'.

Our story begins as a young tank driver in an assault engineer regiment begins to prepare for his role in the Normandy landings.

Many thousands fought and died on D-Day. Everyone who survived has a story to tell – this is mine.

John Smith,
79th Armoured Division

Chapter 1
Death in Dieppe

'It was a fine, clear dawn and we walked right into it. I landed with my regiment in front of the town, where the beach is overlooked at either end by a headland. That meant that the enemy had the entire landing area covered by machine-guns and anti-tank guns, so we were pinned down from the start. Most of us were killed or wounded by the crossfire, and the rest tried to scrape holes for themselves on the beach.

'The air was thick with bullets and there were snipers at work too, picking off the officers. A few men managed to cross the sea wall, but things were no better on the other side. There was a wide promenade and what had been ornamental gardens to cross before you reached the houses, which had all been turned into small fortresses, spitting rifle and machine-gun fire.

'We had a regiment of Churchill tanks with

us which should have been more help. But it just wasn't that simple. The beach consisted of shingle; small, smooth stones that slide about on top of one another. In most cases the tank-tracks just churned the shingle until the tank got bogged down. Some drivers managed to get as far as the sea wall, then found it was too high to cross. There was one place, however, where the tide had piled up the shingle against the wall and a handful managed to get over. They did good work with the houses but they weren't able to break into the town because all the roads were closed off with concrete barricades.

'About that time someone decided that we weren't going anywhere and the raid was called off. I suppose I was lucky. I'd been hit in the legs just after I left the landing-craft and they got me aboard again pretty quickly. Out of my entire company only thirty men made it back to England, and most of them were wounded. They hit us pretty hard.'

The Canadian colonel paused for a moment, recalling the scene of carnage on the Dieppe beach. His audience, including me, John Smith, sat in horrified silence. It was only a couple of days since I'd been sent with a group of others to join this new assault regiment and I still wasn't sure exactly what we were here for. Most of the others had enlisted just after Dunkirk and, because we had worked in the building, construction or heavy-engineering industries, we found ourselves in the Royal Engineers.

We had done some useful work strengthening England's defences against invasion, but as the years went by we began to feel bored. It was now early 1944 and we all knew that we wouldn't be going home until we'd beaten Hitler and his cronies, and that wouldn't happen until we'd invaded German-occupied France to open what was called the Second Front. There just wasn't any sign of that happening and we were starting to get restless. The colonel's lecture on the Dieppe Raid of 1942 was doing nothing to cheer us up. I knew Dieppe had been bad, but I don't think any of us realized just how bad.

'It gets worse,' the colonel continued. 'Since Dieppe the Germans have done a lot to improve their defences right along the Channel coast. They have installed lines of underwater obstacles that remain submerged either side of high tide. These include rows of iron stakes, steel hedgehogs made from girders and triangular constructions we call Element C. These are not only capable of tearing the bottom out of a landing-craft, but they are also fitted with explosive devices.

'The beaches themselves are heavily mined and covered by the fire of machine-guns and artillery weapons housed in concrete bunkers. Where no sea wall exists, the Germans have built high anti-tank walls to block exits from the shore. Behind, there are strong points containing more guns and automatic weapons, protected by mines, wire entanglements and anti-tank ditches, laid out in depth. Houses and other buildings, reinforced with concrete, have also been incorporated into the defences. Herr Hitler is very proud of what he calls his Atlantic Wall, and if we were to attack it in the same way we attacked Dieppe, very few of us would survive.'

A worried murmur rose among the audience.

'This bloke is giving me the willies!' muttered my neighbour, Sapper Joe Hill, known as Gloomy to the rest of us. 'It's just as well they made us make our wills, because the way he's talking someone will be needing them!'

'There is a positive side to all this,' said the colonel, observing the effect his words were having. 'Dieppe *was* bad, but it's over and done with. We have faced the facts and we know the worst that can happen. We have learned the lessons of Dieppe and we have taken into account what the enemy has done to strengthen his defences. Not only will there be no more Dieppe-style attacks, we believe that we now have the means to smash the Atlantic Wall with very few casualties.

'What I am about to tell you is top secret. You will not discuss it – or the training and equipment you receive – with your families or anyone outside this unit. Anyone who does so will face an instant court martial.'

You could have heard a pin drop in the silence that followed. All eyes were on the colonel as he continued.

'Some time ago our division, that is the 79th Armoured Division, was given the task of producing specialist armoured vehicles that are capable of smashing every aspect of the enemy defences. That task is now complete. The vehicles you will be manning are called Assault Vehicles Royal Engineers, or AVREs for short. They can perform a large number of assault engineering tasks. During your training you will come across other vehicles that have been designed for specific tasks such as mine clearing.

'In action, you will be formed into teams and each team's vehicles will be responsible for a particular part of an operation. Remember, it's results that count. The regiment will first train with the AVREs and will then undertake training with the other troops with whom it is to operate. Once training has been completed, I can promise you that the invasion of France will take place very quickly.'

By now, the colonel had us all on the edge of our seats.

'Like we say on my side of the Atlantic, you and I are into a whole new ball game,' he said. 'What's more, we're playing to win. Good luck, and I want to see you leaving this hall a darn sight happier than when you came in!'

We did.

That afternoon we were introduced to the AVRE, which was unlike anything I had ever seen before. An instructor pointed out its more obvious features.

'As you can see,' he said, 'it's based on the Churchill tank, but it has a specially designed turret.'

'What kind of gun is that?' I asked,

pointing to the wide, snub-nosed barrel protruding from the turret.

'It's not a gun,' he replied. 'It's a 290 mm spigot mortar, known as a petard. It will throw a 40-pound, shaped-charge bomb to a maximum range of 80 yards. The bomb, which we call General Wade's Flying Dustbin, is specially designed to crack open concrete fortifications. The petard is a muzzle-loader – which means, for anyone who doesn't know, from the front end. There is one 7.92 mm BESA machine-gun mounted in parallel with it, and another for the exclusive use of the co-driver.'

'What makes the AVRE so special?' someone asked doubtfully. 'It just looks like another tank to me.'

The instructor chuckled.

'That's what you're here to learn,' he said. 'When you've finished, you'll realize this machine can do just about everything but fly!'

Chapter 2
Men and Machines

Over the next few days we learned a great deal more about the AVRE and what it could do. What made the vehicle so useful were fittings that enabled it to be used for all sorts of assault engineering tasks. For example, the AVRE could carry a fascine, which is a huge bundle of chestnut palings up to 8 feet in diameter and 14 feet wide, that could be dropped into an anti-tank ditch, allowing tanks to cross. It could carry a Small Box Girder (SBG) bridge able to support 40 tons, and lay this across gaps up to 30 feet wide, or place it against a sea wall, thus providing a ramp to enable tanks and other vehicles to leave a beach when no other way existed.

A Bobbin could be fitted which unrolled a carpet of hessian and metal tubing ahead of the vehicle, making a firm track over soft ground and so preventing tanks from getting bogged down. An AVRE could place demolition charges against an obstacle or fortification, then explode them by remote control after it had reversed away. It could push a prefabricated Bailey bridge into position. In some circumstances, it could be fitted with a plough that unearthed enemy mines and pushed them out of the vehicle's path. There seemed to be no end of uses to which the AVRE could be put.

Before the war I had worked for a construction company. I had learned how to handle bulldozers and because of this I had been selected as an AVRE driver. Having driven an AVRE a few times, I could see at once why the Churchill had been chosen for the job. It wasn't fast – at best 15 mph on a good road with the wind behind you, and about 8 mph across country – but that wasn't important. What really counted for us assault engineers, who would have to work under fire and very close to the enemy, was that it was heavily armoured, had a hull roomy enough for mounting all the gadgets we would need and that it was able to cross muddy terrain that would leave any other tank in the world stranded. An added bonus was the sponson hatches in either side of the hull to allow the driver and co-driver to escape quickly if the need arose.

The vehicle was a pleasure to drive. Most tanks are fitted with steering levers, but the Churchill had a tiller bar that responded to the slightest touch. On concrete, you could even make the vehicle spin slowly, with one track going forwards and the other backwards. This was called a neutral turn, but it wasn't encouraged because on heavy going you could lose a track. Maintenance, on the other hand, was hard work. At the end of the day, for example, as the driver I had to grease the twenty-two bogie-wheels that formed the tank's suspension, as well as all my other tasks. A crew, however, is a team and everyone mucked in to help me.

Each AVRE was manned by a crew of five, or sometimes six, depending upon what we were doing. We were split into crews early on in our training. My good mate Gloomy was my co-driver. He had worked for the same company as me, in the maintenance and stores department. We had enlisted at the same time and been together ever since. Although of average height, he had a gangling appearance, his arms hanging loosely at his sides, like a gorilla's. He had been nicknamed Gloomy because he took a very serious view of life; he never laughed and always saw the worst in every situation. Apart from that, he was a really decent bloke who would do anything for you. Often, I would read on orders that I was down for guard duty and go back to the billet to find Gloomy shining up my best boots. He was responsible for loading the petard, as well as manning the hull machine-gun in action. Of course, he was not pleased to learn that he would have to slide back his hatch to reload the petard.

'Just my luck to get a muzzle-loader!' he said. 'How long d'you think I'll last, popping in and out like a jack-in-the box?'

'You can't fire a bomb like that from an ordinary breech-loading gun,' replied Sergeant Ron Boyce, our vehicle commander. 'It would explode in the barrel. Anyway, most of the time you'll be reloading under cover, and one quick movement is all you'll need.'

'Suppose there isn't any cover?'

'Stop your moaning!' snarled Ron. 'How d'you think the infantry feel, out there in nothing thicker than their battledress? You'll be snug behind armour plate for 99.9 per cent of the time. Anyway, you can only have your head blown off once!'

'It's the only head I've got,' said Gloomy unhappily.

Ron Boyce was a hard-bitten, long-service regular. He seemed a lot older than the rest of us, although there couldn't have been more than a few years in it. He had the regular soldier's spare, stocky frame. He had seen service on the North-west Frontier of India, cleared mines under fire during the Battle of Alamein, and fought in Tunisia, Sicily and Italy. He was tough, stood no nonsense and was completely fair. We trusted him enough to know that he would never put Gloomy at risk unless he had to, for the very good reason that the petard would be useless without a loader.

Ron and Gloomy were the only two of my team I'd known before joining the regiment. The rest of them I got to know slowly over the first few weeks of training. Our wireless operator was Jock McCabe. Jock came from Glasgow and was small, dark and skinny and had worked as a casual labourer on building sites. He hadn't much self-confidence when he joined up and, perhaps because of that, he had a manner that was half boastful and half mocking. It took a bit of getting used to. Anyway, someone had spotted the intelligence beneath it all and he had been selected for signals training. It was the first time anyone had trusted him, and it meant a lot to him.

'Ye need real brain power tae operate a set,' he would say. 'Me, ah'm noted for it. Now, you're a great bunch o' fellers, but ah'm sorry, ye're no quite up tae it!'

We let him get away with it because he really was good at his job, and we even got to like him.

Mike Emerson, the petard gunner, was a very different type. Mike was tall, fair-haired, of athletic build and very much the gentleman of the crew. His father was a partner in a firm of London surveyors and wanted Mike to follow him into the business. Mike was halfway through his training when war broke out. By then he'd decided he would rather be an actor than a surveyor. Despite his education, he had refused to be considered for a commission when he was called up. He told me that he didn't want the responsibility.

He was good company, always singing songs from musicals or quoting funny extracts from plays, but he was also naturally lazy. Ron Boyce chased him round until he started to shape up and we did the rest, because you can't afford passengers in

17

a tank crew. Once we had hammered into him that we depended on him as much as he did on us, he buckled to and began to achieve excellent results with the petard on the firing range. Mike and Jock hadn't got on to start with because of their very different backgrounds, but in due course they got used to each other.

The sixth member of the crew was Corporal George Meade, who served as demolition NCO, responsible for any charges we might be required to place against enemy fortifications. George had been a quarryman, and his expertise with explosives had resulted in his early promotion. He was a red-faced, burly countryman, quietly spoken, slow and very methodical, as you'd expect from someone in his job. Nothing pleased him more than a really big explosion. Although he would only accompany us when he was needed, he did his share of the work and really pulled his weight.

We settled down to work as a team. It was hard work, too. There were so many different ways an AVRE could be used and we had to learn them all. We practised making fascines from brushwood and chestnut palings. At first we just couldn't seem to get it right. The huge bundles kept bursting out of their chains and collapsing all over the place. The crew of the next AVRE were having similar problems and I thought we might get better results by working together. After the failure of our third attempt I mentioned my idea to Ron.

'I don't think we're getting the chains tight enough, sarge. Let's try passing them round the fascine and attaching the ends to two AVREs. Then they can pull in opposite directions until the chains are really tight.'

My idea worked, and I got a pat on the back.

The next stage of our training was practising mounting and laying the SBG bridge, day and night in all sorts of weather over all sorts of obstacles. This involved a lot of heavy rigging work with cables and pulleys. It was dangerous because the weight involved was considerable and a mistake could cost someone their life. We were careful at first, taking three times as long to complete a job as it should have taken.

I'd done similar work when I was with the construction company, which gave me a slight advantage. Faced with a sagging and lopsided bridge, I was able to point out one or two things we could do during the preliminary stages of rigging to prevent the problem. After consulting the manual, Ron realized I was right and was again impressed. Once competent with the SBG, we started on the demolition frames, called Goat and Onion, which were George Meade's speciality. Finally, we tried out the Bobbin carpet-layer and the Bullshorn mine-plough.

After weeks of hard work mastering the AVREs, the squadron commander, Major Tunstall, announced during morning parade that we would be moving to Norfolk for the next phase of our training.

'The powers that be,' he said, 'are satisfied that you can handle your vehicles and equipment to the required standard. Now, for the first time, we shall be working with the same people we'll be fighting alongside. Part of the training will involve exercises with live ammunition, so keep your wits about you and expect a few surprises.

'Make no mistake about it, this phase of our training will be dangerous. People may be killed or injured. You can reduce the risks by keeping your minds on the job in hand at all times.'

I felt a strange feeling in the pit of my stomach. It wasn't just the dangerous nature of the training; I had been expecting that: it was also the sudden realization that I had passed a major milestone on the road into battle and the understanding that there could be no turning back now.

Chapter 3
Building the Team

When we got to Norfolk we met the regiment who were to be our long-term partners, the South Galloway Horse, equipped with Sherman Crabs. These Crabs were another revelation to us. They were Sherman tanks with a revolving drum mounted on hydraulic arms fitted to the front. The drum was driven by the main engine, and attached to it were chains that flailed the ground ahead of the vehicle, exploding mines in its path. By doing this, it was possible to clear a lane through a minefield at about one-and-a-quarter miles per hour. When it wasn't flailing, the Crab could fight as a normal gun tank.

Training began the day after our arrival. The training area contained accurate reproductions of the obstacles and fortifications we would encounter when we landed in France. We were split into teams and tackled each obstacle in turn. The Crabs would flail their way up to them, then we would arrive to put in a fascine or an SBG bridge, or to place a demolition charge. Then we would repeat the whole exercise, but under fire from machine-guns and with explosions near by to simulate shellfire. It taught us to work together closely, and it gave us some idea of what the fighting would be like.

Ron was the only one in our team who had been in action, so we all valued and respected his opinion.

'How realistic is this, sarge?' I asked him while we were enjoying a brew of tea between exercises. 'I mean, is this the sort of thing we can expect in battle?'

His face became hard and reflective.

'In battle, all you can expect is the unexpected,' he replied. 'Allow for it, and you'll survive. Having said that, the odds are on our side because the training we're getting is the best. What's more, having seen the sort of defences the enemy uses, I can tell you that our equipment should be up to the job.'

Our training with the South Galloway Horse continued for a number of weeks until we began to feel pretty confident in ourselves.

One day I was working on the engine when Jock called to me from the turret.

'Hey, Johnnie, Mr Francis wants a word wi' ye!'

I walked over to where the troop leader was standing with Ron. We exchanged salutes.

'You're shaping up well, Smith,' said the officer. 'You seem to know what you're doing and your crew have confidence in your judgement. We'd like you to sew these on.'

He handed me a pair of lance-corporal's stripes. I gaped at them stupidly for a minute.

'Thank you, sir,' I said eventually.

'They're worth an extra three shillings and sixpence a week to you,' said Ron, 'so don't go mad in the canteen tonight!'

They say that being a lance-corporal is one of the most difficult jobs in the Army. You have the responsibility of seeing that orders are carried out and also have to give orders to men who used to be your equal. Ron, of course, had recommended my promotion. When I got back to the rest of the crew I was a little nervous about how they'd react to the news. It was unusual to be promoted so quickly and I had been surprised myself.

Their reaction was mixed. George was a

corporal and so not really affected by it. Gloomy, however, didn't know what to make of our new relationship, while Mike and Jock weren't too keen on taking orders from me. I was disappointed by this, but I didn't want to lose their friendship. Thinking over the problem later that night, I decided that my only course of action would be to prove that I was worth the stripe I'd been given.

Now we had been together many weeks, word had got round the Army about the unusual equipment being used by the 79th Armoured Division. People were starting to nickname us 'The Funnies'. I knew the division was commanded by Major-General P. C. S. Hobart, but I didn't really know anything about him. During a tea break one day I took the opportunity to question Ron.

'He's the country's leading expert on armoured warfare. He began as an engineer, like us,' he said. 'He was in the Bengal Sappers and Miners – he must have been good, because they don't take just anyone. He was captured by the Turks during the last war and rescued by some of our armoured cars. They say that's why he transferred to the Royal Tank Regiment. He set up the Desert Rats in Egypt just before the war, then got sacked when he fell out with his bosses. After that he joined the Home Guard and they made him a lance-corporal.'

We all laughed.

'Anyway, Churchill wasn't having that. He was recalled and commanded 11th Armoured Division for a while. Then he was given this job, forming a specialist armoured division for the invasion of France. Now it's the biggest division in the Army and it's spread all over the country. They reckon he's covering a thousand miles a week, visiting units by plane and staff car.'

'Sounds like a human dynamo,' I said. 'What's he like?'

Ron shrugged.

'He's got a brilliant mind – most of the ideas behind our vehicles are his. In other respects, people seem to love him or hate him. He's got a fiendish temper and he'll use it on anyone, even if they're senior to him. They say he can't stand fools, so you lot had better stay out of his way unless you want roasting alive!'

Despite Ron's comments, I thought I would like to meet such a remarkable man. I knew we were near the end of our training so I didn't hold much hope of meeting him. Two days later, while we were engaged in general maintenance and replenishment of our vehicles, a group of officers came striding on to the tank park. I almost laughed with disbelief as I realized it was Hobart followed by brigadiers, colonels and the rest of his staff.

'Crews front!' shouted the sergeant-major as Major Tunstall hurried to meet his visitor. By the look on Tunstall's face, it was a surprise visit.

We all stood rigidly to attention in front of our vehicles – all except Gloomy, who obviously hadn't heard and continued to stow petard ammunition. I tried to catch his attention but he was oblivious. The general walked down the line, asking questions here and there. He was shorter than I'd expected and he had the sort of face you don't forget in a hurry – a hawkish nose above a bristling moustache; an aggressive chin; thick, beetling eyebrows and fierce eyes that bored into you from behind thin-rimmed spectacles.

He spotted Gloomy and walked slowly and deliberately towards him. Gloomy glanced up. The general was wearing a trench coat that concealed his badges and he had on his regiment's black beret rather than his red-banded brass hat, so Gloomy must have taken him to be a visiting war correspondent.

'Having a look round?' he said.

'Something like that,' said the general.

The numerous staff officers gave a sharp intake of breath, expecting the general to explode with anger. They probably all saw an immediate end to their military careers. I glanced round. Gloomy and the general were staring into each other's faces, only inches apart. Gloomy was completely at ease and the general, if anything, seemed slightly puzzled. Gloomy showed him a round of petard ammunition.

'We call this General Wade's Flying Dustbin,' he said.

'I know,' said the general.

'The explosive inside is shaped to focus on one point,' continued Gloomy.

'I know that, too,' said the general.

'It will crack open almost any thickness of concrete,' said Gloomy.

'So I believe,' said the general.

At this point Gloomy became almost confidential.

'You know, someone should tell Hitler he's wasting his time with that Atlantic Wall of his. Once we get over there, we're going to smash it apart!'

'I agree with everything you say,' said the general. 'Where are you from?'

'Sevenoaks,' said Gloomy. 'How about you?'

'What? Oh, all over the place!'

'My name's Joe Hill but they call me Gloomy,' said Gloomy shaking the general's hand warmly.

'Mine's Hobart and they call me lots of things!'

The general, deciding that enough was enough, turned and began walking away.

'So long! Don't let them muck you about!' called Gloomy.

'I never do!' said the general, with the ghost of a twinkle in his eye.

Major Tunstall, ashen-faced, saluted as smartly as his shaking limbs would allow.

'Well done!' said the general. 'Morale in this squadron is sky high – keep it that way!'

'That was the divisional commander you were talking to, Hill!' snarled Major Tunstall after the staff cars had left. Gloomy seemed pleasantly surprised rather than impressed.

'Was it, sir? He seems like a really nice bloke – very intelligent, too!'

The major spread his hands in despair as we all dissolved into laughter.

Later that day the major told us that when we landed in France we would be fighting alongside the Canadians. For the last few days of training the combined Crab/AVRE teams did a series of exercises with their infantry regiments, just to show them how we worked and the sort of help we could give them. Like the rest of us, they were impatient to get on with the war. The impression I got was that they were tough customers who would give the Germans a hard time.

After less than a week with the infantry, we were told that that stage of our training was over. Within hours of Major Tunstall's announcement, we were on our way to Dorset. There seemed to be a new sense of urgency in the regiment and I wondered just how close we were to going into battle. Our new location was simply a field near the coast. We slept in canvas bivouacs, pitched against the side of our vehicles. The weather was now much warmer and we got used to living in the open, just as we would have to do when the invasion started.

A day or two after we arrived we had just finished cooking our evening meal on the petrol stoves when we heard tanks moving into the next field. Mike walked over to the hedge.

'They've got propellers!' he shouted in

surprise. 'There's an entire squadron of Shermans here, all fitted with propellers!'

'Pull the other one, sunshine!' said Ron, who had been detailed as the night's guard commander. 'I'm not in the mood for daft jokes!'

'And they've got big canvas skirts!' continued Mike.

'Sometimes, ah worry about you!' said Jock. 'Ye spend so long peerin' intae that gunsight o' yourn ye're startin' tae see things!'

'It's a bad sign when you start seeing things,' said Gloomy, joining the conversation. 'You should report sick and get some pills before it gets worse. You could have caught something really nasty!'

I walked over to the hedge to have a look for myself. The Shermans were exactly as Mike had described them.

'Hi, fellers!' called a cheery Canadian sergeant. 'Why don't you step over and take a look?'

Mike and I found a gap in the hedge and went through. A couple of minutes later Ron, Jock, Gloomy and George followed

'Welcome to the world of the Sherman DD!' said the sergeant. 'DD stands for Duplex Drive, by the way. As you can see, we've got two 26-inch propellers mounted at the rear of the tank, and when we erect the flotation screen we're fully amphibious!'

'You mean that canvas screen will keep a 30-ton tank afloat at sea?' asked Mike.

'Sure will,' said the sergeant, and proceeded to show us how it was erected. 'The screen is made from heavy rubberized canvas. It's mounted on a collapsible steel framework that's welded to the tank. We erect it by pumping compressed air into thirty-six rubber pillars that inflate like long, thin balloons and lift the frame. Once that's upright, we lock it in position with steel struts. Takes about fifteen minutes, that's all.'

'How are the propellers driven?' I asked.

'They're geared to the tracks. They'll give us five or six miles an hour in the water and we steer by changing their direction.'

'That's really ingenious, but how do the DDs fit in with our invasion plans?' I asked.

'The divisional commander reckons that while you boys with the AVREs and the flails are doing your stuff, you could use a little extra gunfire support,' replied the sergeant. 'The idea is that we get launched from our LCTs some way off the beaches. We swim ashore until we reach the shallows. Then we collapse the screen, which we can do quickly.

After that, we fight as ordinary gun tanks and, hopefully, we'll pick off anyone who's causing trouble for you.'

Most of us thought the idea was brilliant, yet another example of the remarkable way Major-General Hobart seemed to think of everything. As usual, however, Gloomy had his own views.

'Sounds like suicide to me,' he said. 'What happens if the sea is rough? You blokes won't stand a chance.'

'Nor will you if don't stop your moanin'!' snapped Ron angrily. 'What's your hobby when you're at home – going to funerals?'

'He's got a point,' said the Canadian. 'That's something we've thought about, too, so we've all had escape training at the submarine school in Gosport.'

He pulled out some equipment from one of the tank's stowage bins and demonstrated how it was used.

'You put this clip on your nose, then you put this mouthpiece between your teeth. The mouthpiece is connected to a short hose that leads into this air bag, which looks a bit like a gas mask. If the tank is going down you open the valve and breathe normally. Then you open the hatch, float to the surface and wait for a rescue boat.'

'You still wouldn't get me in one of those!' said Gloomy.

'They wouldnae have ye, so don't worry yer heed!' said Jock.

The next morning the Canadians gave us a full demonstration of the Sherman DDs in action. With the flotation screens erected, only their tracks suggested that there was a tank inside and, when they took to the water, so little of the screens showed that they looked like ships' lifeboats. They moved out into deep water, then formed two lines to simulate an assault landing. The first line reached the shallows, dropped its shields and fired a couple of blank rounds. The second was closing in when I noticed that one of the tanks was lagging behind. It had taken on a list and I could see water pouring over the edge of the screen.

Suddenly, all hell broke loose. The Canadian officers began shouting. The rescue boat raced to the spot, but before it could arrive the DD had vanished. Four heads broke the surface amid a welter of bubbles. As they were hauled aboard the rescue boat, there was more shouting and a frogman jumped into the water. I realized that something was terribly wrong. The Sherman carried a five-man crew, but only four had come up. Someone was trapped in the sunken tank.

I had to do something. Swimming on that part of the coast can be very dangerous because the beach shelves steeply and there are strong undertows that can carry you off. But I had qualified for my life-saving badge before I joined the Army and I couldn't just watch things happen. I ran to the water's edge and plunged in. I covered the 40 yards to the scene at a rapid crawl. Taking a deep breath, I headed straight down through the line of rising bubbles. Visibility wasn't good, but the bubbles guided me.

I spotted the frogman trying to free the co-driver, caught by a strap on the hatch. Although the co-driver had his breathing apparatus on, he was starting to panic and had grabbed hold of the frogman, making things much worse. Pulling my clasp knife from my pocket, I began sawing at the tangled strap. By the time I had cut through it my lungs were bursting and I was becoming light-headed. Together, the frogman and I heaved the driver out. I got behind him, kicking out for the surface, which seemed far above. For a second, I thought we wouldn't make it, then hands were hauling us into the rescue boat.

It took several minutes for me to get my breath back, so I could only nod while the Canadians slapped me on the back and thanked me. The man we had saved said his name was Ted Cross and if I'd care to look him up in Red Deer, Alberta, after the war, we'd have the biggest party the world had ever seen. The boat put me ashore. Major Tunstall and the lads were waiting for me, ready to shake my hand. I began to feel very cold, but the lads produced towels, dry clothes and hot, sweet tea which did me a power of good.

'Thought we'd seen the last of you,' said Gloomy, sadly.

'Ye know something, Gloomy?' said Jock. 'Ye'd make a fabulous undertaker! Why don't ye give it a try when this is over?'

'Good idea,' said Gloomy, nodding slowly. 'I think I will. Thanks.'

'Well, we know one thing now,' said Ron, 'these machines aren't perfect.'

During all the chaos I hadn't really had time to think about the accident. Ron was right. If this sort of thing could happen during training, what sort of horrors awaited us off the French coast?

Chapter 4
Embarkation

The following day I had recovered from my near drowning and was able to join in the final stages of training. The team seemed unusually quiet and I knew yesterday's accident had worried everyone. We all got on with the job though, spending some time getting our vehicles aboard LCTs and landing them on different types of beaches. We had to reverse into the LCTs so that we could drive straight out into action. It wasn't easy, because whatever the AVRE was carrying made it nose-heavy; the SBG bridge was a particularly awkward load, however well it was rigged. Add to this the fact that the driver, having no rear vision at all, was forced to rely on other people's hand signals, and you'll have some idea how tricky it could be in a confined space.

When training eventually finished, we were sent on a week's embarkation leave.

Although I needed the rest, I found it hard to relax. I couldn't help thinking about what was to come and, after more than a week sleeping in a field, I found the comforts of home unsettled me. Dad understood, because he'd fought in the 1914–18 war, but Ma spent the entire week fussing round me.

During my leave, I paid a duty call on my great-aunt Lavinia. She had been a real beauty in her day and had married a diplomat. She still seemed to inhabit a world of receptions and balls, held long, long ago in the royal palaces of Europe, and to me her equally aged friends seemed just as odd. She was an impressive figure, though, with her silver hair piled high and a long silken black dress edged in white lace at the collar and cuffs.

'Well, John,' she said as we sat having tea, 'I expect you'll be off to fight the kaiser very soon.'

'Hitler,' I said. 'His name is Hitler, Great Aunt.'

'It is not!' she snapped sharply. 'It is Wilhelm. People started calling him Bill, but that was only to be expected, even if he was a grandson of Queen Victoria. Detestable man. One of his Zeppelin airships dropped a bomb on Derry and Thom's department store, you know. Quite ruined my day's shopping.'

'That was unforgivable,' I said.

'I'm glad you agree. Tell me, are people still fighting on the Eastern Front?'

'Yes, they are.'

'I see. Well, hopefully the tsar will be able to go home when they get tired of it.'

'I thought the tsar was murdered by the Bolsheviks in 1918?' I said.

She gave me one of her knowing looks.

'I am going to let you into a great confidence. You must tell no one – not even this Mister Gloomy you keep talking about. Such a strange name.'

'I promise.'

'The tsar and his family are living secretly in Bexleyheath! Cornelia Anson has seen them out for a spin in their motor-car – *twice*!'

'Good Lord!' I said, hoping I sounded sufficiently impressed.

'Not only that, Cornelia bumped into the tsarina in the chemist's the other day! Naturally, she curtsied and made herself known, but the tsarina pretended not to recognize her and left the shop immediately. Can't be too careful in her position, I suppose.'

'No. I expect Bexleyheath is just the sort of place the Bolsheviks would be looking for her,' I said without conviction.

'The dispenser said she was suffering from athlete's foot,' remarked Great-aunt Lavinia after a moment's thought.

'Who? Cornelia Anson?'

'Of course not, you fool – the tsarina! Really, John, you can be so difficult at times!'

I was very fond of my aunt but it was a relief to get back to the comparative sanity of war. As soon as I arrived at base, things began to happen with bewildering speed. Suddenly, the whole of southern England was sealed off. No one was allowed out, outgoing mail was stopped and telephone services were cut off. We began to study photographs, maps and models of our team's landing area, which lay just west of a small resort.

We were briefed thoroughly about the exact plan of attack. The landing would be made just after low tide, when the water was beginning to rise but the lines of enemy obstacles were still exposed. These would already have been dealt with by naval frogmen, who would first disarm the explosive devices then clear 50-yard gaps for the passage of the DDs and the landing-craft. The beach itself was mined and flanked by concrete bunkers containing anti-tank guns and machine-guns. Behind, there was a sea wall and beyond that an anti-tank ditch guarded by yet more bunkers. Finally, there was a row of villas on the coast road, all of which had been turned into miniature fortresses.

It was decided that we would need two Crabs to clear a way through the mines, after which our own AVRE would lay an SBG bridge against the sea wall for the team leader's AVRE to climb over and then drop a fascine into the anti-tank ditch. Next, we would destroy the second line of bunkers and fortified houses with our petards. We were also told exactly what the Canadian DDs and infantry would be doing while we were working.

We could not have been better prepared, but there was still plenty to do. There were maps, lists of wireless frequencies and codes to be studied. The vehicles were stowed with everything we would need, including ammunition, drinking water, rations, bivouacs and personal kit. When the order to move came, we headed for Poole, only a few miles away. The roads

41

were packed with British, Canadian and American tanks, guns and convoys of trucks, all heading for the coast. It could have resulted in endless traffic jams but, like everything else about this operation, it was beautifully organized and everyone kept moving.

In Poole we topped up our fuel tanks, then reversed into the waiting LCT. We had barely finished shackling the vehicles securely when the ramp went up and we were going astern into the harbour. We headed out under a lowering grey sky into a choppy sea to drop anchor amid countless other craft in an assembly area off the coast. Few of us spoke and I realized that, like me, everyone was busy with their own thoughts. We were on our way and there could be no turning back. The only way home lay through France.

Looking round at the others on deck, the black thought struck me that not all of us would be coming home, and some of those who did would be badly injured. I shook it off and started to think about my own role. I told myself that I had been thoroughly trained and knew exactly what I had to do when we reached the other side. I was confident that I could do my job without letting the others down, but the longer we swung at anchor the more I thought of the many things that could go wrong.

Chapter 5

Into Battle

I was standing at the rail of the landing-craft with Gloomy and the rest of the lads. Some of them had managed the odd nap, but for most of us sleep had been impossible because we were too keyed up. The Channel was rough, pitching and rolling the craft. We had been keen and ready to go, but the ship's motion, combined with the smell of fuel and greasy cooking, had turned many a stomach. We had been expecting the order to sail for the French coast, but the sea conditions had only improved enough for it to be given yesterday evening. By then, seasickness had taken its toll. The thought of food revolted us and no one felt much like fighting a battle.

'Just my luck,' said Gloomy. 'This is the worst midsummer weather in the Channel for years, so they decide to start the invasion in the middle of it.'

'Just think of the great time you're having!'

I replied. There was no point in sympathizing with Gloomy; it just made him worse. In fact, once we got under way, the craft's motion seemed to improve a little, or perhaps we were just getting used to it.

Large numbers of aircraft had been passing overhead since the early hours of the morning. Fighter squadrons patrolled incessantly to keep the Luftwaffe at a safe distance while, higher still, huge formations of bombers headed south to give the enemy yet another pounding. I could hear the tremendous crash and blast of sound as the battleships and cruisers began their bombardment of the French coast. The scene which met our eyes in the growing light was incredible. We knew that a large number of ships had been assembled for the invasion, but none of us imagined how many. They covered the entire surface of the sea, from one horizon to the other. There were battleships and cruisers, belching great clouds of flame and smoke whenever their guns fired, destroyers by the dozen, minesweepers, supply ships and landing-craft of every type you can think of, many of them towing barrage balloons. It was the most awe-inspiring sight. In an instant I forgot my seasickness and tiredness – I knew that I was watching history being made.

'Will you look at that!' I said. 'One day we'll tell our grandchildren about this!'

'There's France,' said Gloomy, pointing ahead.

A dark smudge of land had appeared above the tossing grey water. From it thick columns of smoke were rising from the red glow of fires towards the overcast sky. Our escorting destroyers went into action, adding to the din with their gunfire. The ship's loudspeaker system crackled into life.

'D'ye hear there! Troops return to the tank deck. Remove shackles and switch on wireless sets. Do not, repeat *not*, start engines until ordered.'

'This is it,' I thought to myself. 'This is what they call the moment of truth.' I could feel my heart beginning to pound at twice the usual rate and I started breathing deeply to bring it back under control.

On the tank deck we set about removing the chains that had kept our vehicles securely shackled down during the voyage. There were four tanks in our team. First out would be two Sherman Crabs of the South Galloway Horse, followed by my own AVRE, carrying a box-girder bridge that overhung the Crabs, and finally the team commander, Captain Holroyd, our squadron's second-in-command, in an AVRE with a fascine mounting. We could hear the wireless operators checking their net inside the turrets.

'Delta Two-Three Charlie, loud and clear, over.'

'Delta Two-Three Charlie, loud and clear, roger, out.'

Our own wireless was working properly. That was no surprise, as Jock was good at his job, even if he did keep telling you so all the time.

I could see the landing-craft's steel-helmeted gunners taking up their positions behind their 20 mm cannon. A party of seamen hurried past, heading for the bow ramp.

'All the best, lads!' shouted one of them.

There was an explosion near by that made the craft's hull ring. We were drenched with falling water. More explosions followed and I realized we must be coming under fire from the shore batteries. I had an icy, hollow feeling in my stomach and my limbs seemed to lose their power.

All of a sudden the tank deck, with all its smells and discomfort, seemed like home.

Just for a few seconds I wanted to stay there. I was experiencing real fear for the first time. I glanced round nervously but everyone else looked fine. I closed my eyes and quickly tried to get myself under control. Captain Holroyd, who had seen active service in Italy, seemed to sense the fear.

'Waiting is always the worst part,' he said quietly as he walked along the line of tank crews. 'Once it starts we'll all be too busy to think about anything but the job we're doing.'

He pointed towards the bows.

'Remember, everyone, the only way home is down that ramp!'

The loudspeaker crackled again as the LCT's skipper came on.

'D'ye hear there! We shall be touching down in approximately seven minutes. Good luck to you all!'

'Mount – drivers start up!' shouted Holroyd.

We clambered aboard our vehicles. I turned the ignition switch, then pressed the starter. To my intense relief, the engine fired first time. I had been having nightmares about the AVRE not starting, leaving us and half the assault team stranded aboard the LCT. Blue exhaust fumes began to fill the tank deck. Lines of tracer from the craft's 20 mm cannon began snaking overhead towards the shore.

The next command came over the wireless.

'Hallo, all stations Delta Two, close down. Gunners load and make safe. Out.'

Beside me, Gloomy reached up and thrust a bomb into the muzzle of the 290 mm petard mortar; then he opened the cover of the BESA hull machine-gun, fed in a belt of ammunition, closed the cover, cocked the gun and applied the safety catch. With a thumping sound, all the AVREs' hatches were slammed shut, leaving us in semi-darkness.

The next few minutes seemed the longest in my life. I couldn't see a lot through my visor, but I kept my eyes glued to it. I could see the seamen preparing to lower the bow ramp. There was a small explosion on the turret roof of the leading Crab.

'They've opened up with their mortars,' said Ron over the intercom. 'Now you can see why we've closed down.'

The bomb didn't seem to bother the Crab's crew, but I saw one of the seamen get hit by a flying splinter. Two of his friends dragged him out of the way.

Although I had the handbrake on I felt the suspension shift slightly and knew we had reached the shoreline. The increased vibration transmitted upwards through the steel deck told me that the skipper had his engines at full ahead to keep the craft safely grounded while the tanks disembarked, just as we had practised on exercises. Then the bow ramp began to drop. With a puff of exhaust smoke the leading Crab started down it, its chains thrashing madly as soon as it reached the shallows. The second Crab followed.

Because of the heavy, awkward load we were carrying I wanted to give them plenty of room before I moved off.

'Driver – advance!' barked Ron.

I selected first gear, released the handbrake and let in the clutch. Squealing, the vehicle began to move forward, the SBG bridge swaying heavily from side to side. Ahead lay the ramp and beyond that the moment we had been training hard for during the past six months. Would it pay off? Was the confidence we had built in ourselves and our equipment justified? At that moment, all I knew for certain was that beyond the ramp lay death and destruction.

Chapter 6
The Atlantic Wall

I steered the AVRE carefully through the bows of the landing-craft. The two Crabs were now crawling up the beach, one behind and to the right of the other. Every so often there was an explosion as one of their chains detonated a mine. I estimated that they had about 70 yards to go before they reached the sea wall. My hands were sticky on the controls and I knew I was sweating hard. My heart was still pounding away and my breathing was much faster. I was badly frightened but inside me there was a small angry voice nagging away: 'Go on – you know what to do!' it kept saying. 'You've been told often enough – just get on with it!' There was no other choice, so that's what I did.

The LCT had brought us in exactly opposite our objective. Ahead of me I could see the sea wall against which I had to lay my SBG bridge. Beyond that I could see the line of houses, just as we had seen them on the photographs and models we had used during training. They had seemed harmless enough then, but now the entire area looked ugly and full of menace. The air was full of drifting smoke. There were shells bursting everywhere, and I knew that those exploding on the beach had been fired by the enemy's guns and mortars. On what had been the promenade there was a dense entanglement of barbed wire that would have proved fatal to an unsupported infantry attack.

From various points in the houses I could see the flicker of machine-guns firing. To our left, out of my line of vision, was the bunker complex we had been warned about. I was gripped by a sudden fear that our DDs hadn't touched down and that we would be at the mercy of its anti-tank gunners. Behind the bunkers was the little seaside resort, which we now knew was called St Jacques-sur-Mer. Along the beach to our right there was another bunker complex, but that was the responsibility of the neighbouring team and I couldn't afford to think about it. Ron had told me many times that war is a very local thing – all you can do is concentrate your attention on what is going on in your immediate area.

In the few seconds during which I had absorbed these impressions we had reached the head of the ramp. One of the sailors gave us the thumbs-up.

'Easy, now,' said Ron's voice in my headphones.

I stayed in bottom gear and kept my eyes on the rev counter, maintaining a steady supply of power to the engine. As we descended the ramp the bridge nodded forward, as I knew it would, pulling the nose of the vehicle down. I eased back on the throttle until we levelled out in the shallows, then increased power slowly but steadily as we crawled out on to the beach. In my visor, the two Crabs came back into view, flailing steadily with the leader some 30 yards from the sea wall.

'Well done,' said Ron. 'Away you go.'

I nervously followed the lane cleared by the Crabs. We were now under heavy machine-gun fire. I could see sparks flying off the Crabs, and off our own bridge as well. Like most tank men, I only used one of my headphones because the constant mush of sound stays with you long after the set has been switched off, so I could clearly hear the enemy bullets striking our armour. I realized then how important the live ammunition training had been.

There was a flash against the side of the leading Crab. Almost immediately it began belching smoke and flames. As the crew scrambled out, one of them was hit and the others dragged him into cover behind the vehicle.

'It takes about seven seconds for a Sherman to brew,' said Ron grimly. 'Just be glad we're based on the Churchill – that takes a lot longer.'

The second Crab continued to flail its way up to the sea wall, then swung hard left to make some space for us. It stopped flailing and opened fire on the bunker that had knocked out its team-mate.

'Stay in his tracks,' said Ron as we lumbered slowly up the cleared lane. 'Steer as close to the brew-up as you can – never mind if the paintwork gets a good scorching.'

I made a steering adjustment to the right and centred up. The bridge swayed dangerously, threatening to pull us off the narrow course I had set. As we passed the blazing wreck I could feel the heat from it inside the driving compartment. We were now near the sea wall, but when to lay the bridge was Ron's decision. I slowed to a crawl.

'Halt!' he said sharply.

The front of the bridge was now overhanging the promenade railings. The internal release gear was pulled and the bridge dropped.

'Reverse – halt!'

I could see that we had made a good, clean drop and that the climb did not present too much of a challenge to a trained tank driver. In its fall, the bridge had flattened a section of railings.

'Over you go!' said Ron.

I engaged bottom gear and moved forward, keeping the revs high. Freed from the weight of the bridge, the AVRE seemed incredibly light to handle. We began to climb at an angle of about 30 degrees. For a while, all I could see in my visor was sky. When the nose began to drop I kept the power on until we landed firmly on the promenade, then halted as soon as the anti-tank ditch came into view. The houses seemed much closer and were spitting fire. To judge from the racket outside, we seemed to be everyone's target.

'Mike, Gloomy, what are you waiting for?' snarled Ron into the intercom. 'Sort 'em out with your BESAs!'

The two machine-guns began pouring streams of tracer into the houses through every window and door. We seemed to be winning, when I spotted a flash in the basement of one of the houses. The next second the AVRE lurched as something struck the front armour with terrific force. We were under fire from an anti-tank gun.

'Anyone spot him?' shouted Ron.

'He's under the house with green shutters,' I said. 'You can see a line of concrete where they've turned the basement into a bunker – got it?'

'Yes. Mike, bring the house down on top of him!'

There was a second impact while Mike was laying the petard on to his target. I was truly grateful for the Churchill's stout armour, but wondered how long it would be before the German gunner did us some real damage. At last the petard gave its peculiar metallic cough. I watched the bomb curving its way through the air. It struck the house just under the roof. There was a tremendous explosion and most of the front wall collapsed. When the dust cleared, the anti-tank gun's fire slit had vanished under tons of rubble.

'Nice one!' said Ron.

'I suppose you want me to reload,' said Gloomy resignedly.

I could understand his reluctance, as the

AVRE was still under fire from several machine-guns.

'Stay where you are for the moment,' said Ron. 'I'm going to chuck out a couple of smoke grenades. John, once they start to build up, move us about 30 yards to the left.'

Under cover of the dense white fog I did as I was told. The rain of bullets on the armour ceased. Gloomy slid back his hatch, shoved a bomb firmly into the muzzle of the petard and closed down again. He seemed very pleased with himself.

The smoke cleared and we came under fire again. To the right I could see Captain Holroyd's AVRE moving towards the anti-tank ditch. The fascine it carried was starting to smoulder, probably because it had been hit by the enemy's tracer bullets. The vehicle paused at the edge of the ditch. I saw the cables go slack as the release gear was pulled, then the driver gave a nudge forward and the smoking bundle toppled forward, filling the gap. The captain's voice came over the radio.

'All stations Delta Two-Three, follow me – out.'

His AVRE crossed the fascine, machine-gunning as it went.

'Follow him,' said Ron.

As I swung right towards the crossing I could see that our team's remaining Crab was also over the sea wall and was being followed by several DDs. The Canadian infantry were also swarming over and fanning out as they ran towards the ditch. As we crossed the fascine the weight of the vehicle crushed out the smouldering fire. I moved up on Captain Holroyd's left just as he sent a bomb sailing towards the house opposite. It struck the corner, bringing down most of two walls and some of the roof as well. We took on the next house. Our bomb disappeared through a window and exploded inside, blowing out most of the upper storey. Gloomy, now more confident, reloaded quickly.

We began to blow the buildings apart systematically, supported by the Crab and the DDs, who fired high-explosive shells into the ruins and combed the surrounding area with their machine-guns.

'I think they've stopped firing,' I said. 'What do you want me to do?'

'Stay where you are,' replied Ron. 'Give someone else a chance!'

The DDs began moving forward. Bayonets fixed, the Canadian infantry ran past, shouting fiercely as they went in for the kill.

Suddenly it was all over. White handkerchiefs were being waved from among the ruins and there were men appearing in all sorts of unexpected places with their hands raised. They were the first Germans I had ever seen. As they came forward to be rounded up and marched off, they seemed dirty, tired, shocked, bewildered and very ordinary – nothing like the brutal, ruthlessly efficient soldiers I had been expecting.

We dismounted to stretch some of the stiffness out of our limbs. We were all surprised and elated that we had come through our first battle alive and unhurt. We were also jubilant that we had won a major victory, smashing our way through the Atlantic Wall exactly according to plan. Near by, Captain Holroyd was talking to a captured officer. The German, his uniform torn and covered with brick dust, was speaking in clipped, precise English.

'We had expected to hold these positions indefinitely. We had no idea that you would invade with armoured vehicles specially designed to break through our defences. You are to be congratulated on your ingenuity!'

'Oh, we've a few more surprises for you!' said Holroyd, chuckling. 'You'd better get down to the beach with your chaps – you don't want to miss a long holiday in England, do you?'

After the breaching teams had completed their tasks, the squadron was to rally near the houses. Most of the AVREs had arrived now, and with them came Mr Francis and the rest of the troop, who had been working with another team. We had suffered some casualties, but the more seriously wounded were already on their way back to England. We had lost three AVREs, including one bogged down, one with mine damage to its tracks, and one knocked out by an anti-tank gun. Not all the teams had been able to break through the defences, as we had, but the planners had left a wide margin for safety. Now infantry, tanks and guns were streaming past us as the fighting moved inland. I looked back at the beach and saw yet more landing-craft coming in, discharging troops, vehicles and stores of every kind until I began to wonder whether there was space for them all.

'Well done, everyone!' said Major Tunstall as he walked round the crews. 'It's pretty clear already that the enemy didn't know what hit them. Makes all that training we did worthwhile, doesn't it?'

'Here comes trouble,' said Gloomy, pointing.

A Jeep containing a Canadian brigadier had just bounced its way over the fascine and was heading straight for us at speed. For once I was inclined to agree with Gloomy. Something had obviously gone wrong and it looked like we were going to have to sort it out.

Chapter 7
Sniper!

Major Tunstall saluted as the Jeep pulled up in a cloud of dust beside us. The brigadier returned the salute and clambered out. He looked pleased with the way things were going, but at the same time there was an urgency about him that suggested he had a problem.

'First, I want to thank you fellows for the way you smashed through those defences,' he said. 'Thanks to you, our casualties are just a tiny fraction of what they were at Dieppe. I can't tell you how grateful I am.'

'It's been a pleasure, sir,' said the major. 'Is there anything else we can do to help?'

'There is one thing,' replied the brigadier, pointing along the sea front. 'There's a ramp leading down to the beach about 250 yards in that direction. Before the war it was used for launching yachts. The whole length of it is choked with dense barbed wire and the top and bottom are closed off with those iron frameworks you call Element C, which have explosive charges attached. It should have been cleared by our own engineers, but their landing-craft has taken a hit and it will take some time for them to sort themselves out. The trouble is, I need that ramp to get our transport moving inland – at the moment the lorries are piling up on the beach. It's not just that they're making a fine target for the German artillery – the tide is starting to come in as well!'

'We'd be glad to help,' replied Major Tunstall. 'Sergeant Boyce, get your team together and see what you can do.'

'Right away, sir,' replied Ron.

I could hear Gloomy grumbling about not having time to rest, but I was quite happy to help out. Keeping busy would hopefully stop me thinking about the danger surrounding us. Ron studied his large-scale map of the area and quickly found the ramp.

'It's marked *Do Not Petard*, sir,' he said.

Major Tunstall nodded.

'That's right – if it's going to be used by wheeled vehicles we can't afford to smash it up. Let's see what Corporal Meade thinks.'

'Hey, Mr Bang!' shouted Jock, using the nickname he had given our demolition NCO.

'We've found somethin' for ye tae do, after all!'

George appeared from round the back of the AVRE. The brigadier explained the problem. George reminded me of a family doctor: the way he asked questions quietly, nodded wisely and finally suggested a solution.

'I'll neutralize the charges on the Element C, sir, then I'll cut the framework at ground level with our own explosives. After that, I'll use Bangalore torpedoes on the wire. That should enable us to tow what's left of the obstacle out of the way.'

'Yes, that's the way I'd tackle it, too,' said the brigadier. 'Right, off you go.'

We drove over to the head of the ramp and began unloading George's explosives, detonators, wires, switch gear and Bangalore torpedoes.

'Ye're the most dangerous man ah ever met!' said Jock. 'Ye sit there, good as gold, sayin' nothing, an' all the time ye've got enough explosive aboard tae wreck half of Europe! Ah'd never hae come, if ah'd known what ye get up tae!'

George simply smiled and began examining the enemy charges on the Element C at the top of the ramp. There was a sudden crack and George's legs seemed to be swept from under him. His helmet struck the promenade railing with a sound we could hear yards away.

'Sniper!' shouted someone. 'Get down!'

We didn't need telling twice. This was a tricky situation. Even if we mounted the vehicle, we couldn't use its heavy weapons because there were so many of our own troops about. I began looking around for a likely spot where the sniper might be hiding.

Some 40 yards away there was what had once been an ornamental shrubbery, just inland from the promenade. It seemed to be at about the same angle from which the shot had come. I quickly drew my revolver. It wasn't much use normally because it was so inaccurate, but I got to my knees and fired all six shots at the shrubbery. If the sniper was there, it might force him to move.

'There he goes!' shouted a Canadian voice.

I had a brief glimpse of a grey figure in a German peaked forage cap. He was visible for only a second, running between the shrubbery and the promenade, then he vanished as though the earth had swallowed him up.

I noticed that every 50 yards or so there were drainage culverts passing under the promenade to empty through holes in the sea wall. They were made from concrete pipes that were large enough to crawl into. I was reasonably certain that the sniper had gone to ground in one of them. I reloaded my revolver. My earlier fear had been replaced by real anger. George was a decent sort and I didn't know whether he'd been badly hit or not.

'Ron, get the boys to cover me!' I shouted. 'Come on, Gloomy, let's go!'

I scrambled up to the turret, took two smoke grenades from the rack and dropped down beside Gloomy. I explained my plan to him. We set off along the promenade, reasonably certain we would be safe as long as we stayed on the roadway. From above, we carefully examined both ends of the culvert we thought the sniper was hiding in.

'The sea wall end is closed by an iron grille,' said Gloomy.

'That means he can only escape through my end. Can you get a grenade through the grille?'

He nodded.

'Right, on the count of three, then get over here fast! One, two, three – now!'

We tossed the grenades into the pipe at the same time. White smoke began to belch out of both ends. I could hear coughing.

'Here he comes!'

Choking, the figure emerged on all fours. Gloomy knocked the remaining air out of his body by landing on him, knees first. At the same time I grabbed his rifle and got a headlock on him. When we hauled him upright we could see that he was only about seventeen years old, with long fair hair swept backwards. We frog-marched him back to the others, who were grinning all over their faces.

'Ah'm takin' guid care no' tae upset you in future, corporal!' shouted Jock. 'Ye're turnin' intae a real desperate character!'

I was pleased to see that George was on his feet, even if he seemed a bit groggy.

The brigadier drew up in his Jeep, obviously worried by the delay.

'Is that the toe-rag who shot the heel off my boot?' asked George, indicating the prisoner. 'For a sniper, you're a rotten shot, sunshine!'

The young German had recovered his breath. He must have realized that we were not going to harm him, because he had assumed a sneering expression.

'You were lucky,' he said. 'Soon your luck will end, because we shall drive you back into the sea! Heil Hitler!'

'I don't think so,' said the brigadier, and turned to one of his infantrymen. 'March this young fool down to the prisoner-of-war cage on the beach, will you?'

'We seem to be getting two sorts of prisoner,' he said after the sniper had been escorted away. 'The older men are mostly glad they're out of it, but some of the young ones are fanatics who'll gladly die for the Führer if they can take some of us with them.'

'I've come across them before, sir,' said Ron. 'Someone in the Hitler Youth tells them they're tough guys and they believe it until we teach them different.'

'I'll carry on with the job, sir, if you don't mind,' said George. 'Let's hope we don't have any more interruptions like the last one!'

'You won't,' replied the brigadier. 'I've arranged for a squad of my boys to look after you – I should have thought of it earlier.'

The rest of us fetched and carried for George while he worked methodically on the obstacles blocking the ramp. At the bottom of it I could see the Canadian lorries lined up and ready to move off. George carefully removed the German explosives from the Element C, wired up his own charges around the base of the girders, then detonated them.

The girders were beautifully cut at ground level, but the Element C just sagged into the barbed-wire entanglement on the ramp. The Canadians below were getting impatient as the tide lapped steadily towards their vehicles. I wondered why they didn't use the SBG bridge we had put in earlier, then realized that was being reserved for tanks and other tracked vehicles.

'Looks a worse mess than when you started,' said Ron.

'Get me the Bangalore torpedoes, will you?' replied George in his leisurely manner. 'I think we'll need all of them.'

The Bangalore torpedo was simply a long tube filled with explosives which could be detonated from a safe distance. We screwed several together and pushed them into the wire entanglement.

'Get down!' shouted George to the Canadians.

The charge went off with a terrific bang. It cut a lot of the wire and generally loosened the entanglement, but George was not satisfied. We inserted another torpedo. This time the explosion spread the wire over a wider area and we could see a lot of it was hanging loose. George gave a grunt of satisfaction.

'One more should do it,' he said.

After the third charge the entanglement was further loosened and much of it was hanging in swathes over the sides of the ramp. We unshackled one end of the towing hawser from the AVRE and fastened it to the girders of the upper Element C, to which large areas of wire were still clinging. A crowd of Canadians appeared with wire cutters, but Ron warned them off as he climbed into the turret.

'Stand well back, lads!' he shouted. 'This stuff will tear you to ribbons if it catches you! Off you go, John, slow and steady.'

I engaged first gear and let in the clutch slowly, increasing the revs as I felt the pull. Something gave, then something else, and slowly we began to move forward, towing a huge tangle of girders, wire and stakes.

'Easy!' shouted Ron suddenly. 'The wire's snapping and snaking about all over the place – it nearly took the head off some poor chap! That's far enough.'

I got out and watched the Canadians swarming over the ramp, cutting away what was left of the wire and removing the Element C from the bottom. As soon as a path was cleared, their transport began leaving the beach, heading inland in an endless stream – vehicles towing artillery and anti-tanks guns, supply lorries, signals trucks, water tankers, Jeeps and motor cycles. The brigadier came across and thanked us, especially George. As he shook our hands I could see the relief on his face.

I noticed Mike was looking rather troubled.

'Anything wrong, mate?' I asked.

'That's a terrific weight of responsibility he's carrying,' he replied quietly. 'Just think of all those blokes relying on him. Suppose we hadn't been able to open the ramp and they'd had to face a counter-attack without enough ammunition.'

'If we hadn't opened the ramp he'd have found another way to get ammunition up to them,' I replied, knowing what was going through Mike's mind. 'That's his job and he has to get on with it. Are you having second thoughts about not applying for a commission?'

'No,' he said quickly. 'I don't want anyone getting killed because of an order I've given.'

I liked Mike but I didn't agree with him, so we left it at that. We got back to the rally point, hoping we would have time for a brew of tea, but it was not to be. Some of the AVREs had been sent back down to the beach to recover fascines and other items from bogged-down vehicles. The rest were clearly on the point of moving off. We joined their crews as Major Tunstall was briefing them.

'The Canadian engineers in St Jacques-sur-Mer are having a spot of bother with some tough guys holed up in the town hall,' he was saying. 'They want to clear a couple of road-blocks, but they can't get near them because the enemy has them covered with machine-guns. Their own tanks are too busy to help them at the moment, but they think we can sort out the problem quickly. Is there anyone here who speaks reasonable German?'

I put up my hand. At the building company I had sometimes worked on imported German machinery. The company needed the manuals to be translated and one reason I had got a job with them was that I had studied German at school and later at evening classes. Old soldiers say you should never volunteer, and I began to wonder whether I had been wise to do so. After all that had happened during the day, I was now being asked to talk some hard-case Germans into surrendering. Nervous exhaustion had dulled the edge of fear, but I began to wonder whether active service was just a case of being thrown into one life-threatening situation after another. At that moment, though, there wasn't any alternative.

HOBO'S FUNNIES — ARMOURED VEHICLES

AVRE with SBG
(Small Box Girder) Bridge

Specification

Crew: Commander, Demolition NCO, Radio Operator, Petard Gunner, Driver, Petard Loader/Co-driver
Weight: 39 tons (excluding bridge)
Length: 24 ft 5 in (7.5 m)
Height: 8 ft (excluding bridge) (2.4 m)
Width: 10 ft 8 in (3.25 m)
Engine: Bedford twin-six 350 hp
Transmission: Merritt-Brown four-speed gearbox
Speed: road - 15.5 mph (25 kph)
      cross country - 8 mph (13 kph)
Fording depth: 3 ft 4 in (1.2 m) without preparation
Vertical obstacle: 2 ft 6 in (.9 m)
Armour: Hull front – 89 mm 101 with applique armour
      Hull sides – 76 mm
      Turret front – 88 mm
      Turret sides – 76 mm
Armament: 290 mm Petard (spigot mortar) capable of throwing two or three 40 lb bombs per minute to a range of eighty yards (seventy-three metres).
1 x 7.92 mm Besa machine gun mounted co-axially
1 x 7.92 Besa machine gun in hull

The SBG bridge could be laid across gaps up to thirty feet (nine metres) wide and had a maximum capacity of forty tons. It could also be placed against a sea wall to provide a ramp enabling vehicles to leave the beach.

Churchill ARK
(Armoured Ramp Carrier)

Specification
A turretless variant of the Churchill gun tank
Crew: Commander, Driver, Co-driver/hull gunner
plus one to assist in ramp handling
Weight: 31 tons (including ramps)
Length: 24 ft 5 in (7.5 m) (excluding ramps)
Height: 6 ft 6 in (2 m)
Width: 10 ft 8 in (3.25 m)
Engine: Bedford twin-six 350 hp
Transmission: Merritt-Brown four-speed gearbox
Speed: road – 15.5 mph (25 kph)
        cross country – 8 mph (13 kph)
Fording depth: 3 ft 4 in (1.2 m) without preparation
Vertical obstacle: 2 ft 6 in (.9 m)
Armour: Hull front – 89 mm 101 with applique armour
        Hull sides – 76 mm
Armament: 1 x 7.92 Besa machine gun in hull

The Churchill ARK was fitted with trackways
built above the vehicle's own tracks and a
folding ramp at the front and rear. It could
be driven against a wall to create a ramp or
into an anti-tank ditch or a crater in a
roadway and used as a bridge by other vehicles.

Churchill Crocodile Flame Thrower

Specification

A variant of the Churchill gun tank Mark VII
Crew: Commander, Radio Operator/Loader, Gunner,
Driver, Flame gunner/Co-driver
Weight: 39 tons (excluding trailer)
Length: 24 ft 5 in (7.5 m) (excluding trailer)
Height: 8 ft (2.4 m)
Width: 10 ft 8 in (3.25 m)
Engine: Bedford twin-six 350 hp
Transmission: Merritt-Brown four-speed gearbox
Speed: road - 15.5 mph (25 kph)
        cross country - 8 mph (13 kph)
Fording depth: 3 ft 4 in (1.2 m) without preparation
Vertical obstacle: 2 ft 6 in (.9 m)
Armour: Hull front -   152 mm
        Hull sides - 76 mm
        Turret front - 152 mm
        Turret sides - 76 mm
Armament: 1 x 75 mm gun
1 x 7.92 mm Besa machine gun mounted co-axially
1 x flame gun in hull, replacing the Besa machine gun

The flame gun could project burning fuel to a
range of ninety yards (eighty-two metres),
although in some conditions 120 yards (110 metres)
was possible. Four hundred gallons of fuel for the
gun was carried in a two-wheeled armoured trailer
weighing 6.5 tons. If damaged, the trailer could
be jettisoned by means of a quick release device.
In such circumstances, or when the flame fuel was
expended, the Crocodile continued to fight as a
conventional gun tank.

AVRE Fascine Carrier

Specification
A variant of the Churchill AVRE
Crew: Commander, Demolition NCO, Radio Operator,
Petard Gunner, Driver, Petard Loader/Co-driver
Weight: 39 tons (excluding fascine)
Length: 24 ft 5 in (7.5 m)
Height: 8 ft (2.4 m)
Width: 10 ft 8 in (3.25 m)
Engine: Bedford twin-six 350 hp
Transmission: Merritt-Brown four-speed gearbox
Speed: road - 15.5 mph (25 kph)
       cross country - 8 mph (13 kph)
Fording depth: 3 ft 4 in (1.2 m) without preparation
Vertical obstacle: 2 ft 6 in (.9 m)
Armour: Hull front - 89 mm 101 with applique armour
         Hull sides - 76 mm
         Turret front - 88 mm
         Turret sides - 76 mm
Armament: 1 x 290 mm Petard (spigot mortar) capable
of throwing two or three 40 lb bombs per minute to
a range of eighty yards (seventy-three metres).
1 x 7.92 mm Besa machine gun mounted co-axially
1 x 7.92 Besa machine gun in hull

The fascine, was up to eight feet (2.5 m) in
diameter and fourteen feet (4.25 m) wide. A
quick-release device enabled it be dropped
accurately into an anti-tank ditch, stream or
crater, allowing other tanks to cross.

Sherman Crab

Specification
A mine-clearing variant of the Medium Tank M4
Sherman.
Crew: Commander, Radio Operator, Gunner, Driver,
Hull Gunner/Co-driver
Weight: 30 tons
Length: 19 ft 10.5 in (6 m) (vehicle only)
Height: 8 ft (2.4 m)
Width: 10 ft 8 in (3.25 m)
Engine: Chrysler multibank 370 hp
Transmission: Manual with five forward and one
reverse gears
Speed: road – 25 mph (40 kph)
          cross country – 15-20 mph (24–32 kph)
          flailing – 1.25 mph (2 kph)
Fording depth: 3 ft (.9 m) without preparation
Vertical obstacle: 2 ft 6 in (.75 m)
Armour: Hull front – 50 mm
        Turret front – 75 mm
Armament: 1 x 75 mm gun
1 x .30 in Browning machine gun mounted co-axially
1 x .30 in Browning machine gun in hull

Two hydraulic arms holding a rotating drum were
mounted on the front of the vehicle. The drum was
fitted with forty-three chains that flailed the
ground ahead of the tank, exploding mines in its
path. It was capable of clearing a lane nine feet
nine inches (three metres) wide through a
minefield and, when not flailing, could fight at
a conventional gun tank.

Sherman DD

Specification

An amphibious variant of the Medium Tank M4
Sherman
Crew: Commander, Radio Operator, Gunner, Driver,
Hull Gunner/Co-driver
Weight: 29.7 to 32.5 tons depending upon Mark
Length: 19 ft 4 in (5.9 m)
Height: 9 ft (2.75 m)
Width: 8 ft 7 in (2.6 m)
Engine & Transmission: Varied according to Mark
Speed: road - 24-29 mph (39-47 kph)
      cross country - 15-20 mph (24-32 kph)
      afloat - 4 knots
Vertical obstacle: 2 ft 6 in (.75 m)
Armour: Turret front - 75 mm
      Hull front - 50 mm
Armament: 1 x 75 mm gun
1 x .30 in Browning machine gun mounted co-axially
1 x .30 in Browning machine gun in hull

DD stands for Duplex drive, reflecting the tank's
amphibious capability. Floatation was provided by
a collapsible canvas screen that was erected by
filling rubber tubes with compressed air, then
locked in place with struts. When afloat, the tank
hung from the screen below water level, being
driven by propellers. On reaching the shoreline
the screen could be collapsed and the vehicle
could go into action as a conventional gun tank.

A landing craft packed with assault vehicles

Major-General P.C.S. Hobart
Commander of the 79th Armoured Division

Chapter 8
Rain of Destruction

Altogether, seven of the squadron's AVREs trundled into St Jacques-sur-Mer along the coast road. On the outskirts we passed modern villas, many of which had been seriously damaged by the warships' bombardment. As we entered the older part of the fishing port the streets became narrow and twisting. From time to time I caught a glimpse of the Canadian infantry, running between firing positions or peering at us from windows. I could see the road ahead opening up into a square, but before we reached it a Canadian officer stepped into the street, holding up his hand.

'Hold it there,' said Ron.

I halted, applied the handbrake and wriggled out of the sponson door. Major Tunstall was talking to the Canadian.

'The town hall is on the far side of the

square, sir,' said the officer. 'They've been using it as their local headquarters and they've made it pretty clear they intend staying put.'

'We'll see about that!' growled the major. 'Come on, Corporal Smith, let's talk some sense into them.' I saw that he had tied a piece of white cloth to a length of aerial rod. We reached the edge of the square and the major pushed his white flag round the corner.

A fierce firefight was taking place between the enemy in the town hall and the Canadians occupying the other three sides of the square. Gradually, in response to shouts of 'Cease firing!', the racket died down. Cautiously we entered the square. Sixty yards of open cobbles separated us from the enemy, and I never felt so exposed in my life.

The town hall was an oblong, three-storey stone building with a broad flight of steps leading up to an ornate pillared porch. What caught my eye immediately were the large red Nazi flags draping the building and a sign in German lettering saying *Kommandantur*. I also noticed that there were sandbagged machine-gun emplacements on the roof, from which heads in coal-scuttle helmets watched us curiously. Every window from attic to basement had also been sandbagged and loopholed. There was another sandbagged machine-gun emplacement at the top of the steps, the bottom of which were closed off with a barbed-wire entanglement. On either side of the building were the concrete anti-tank barriers the Canadians had mentioned, closing off the roads out of the town.

We halted at the entanglement. One of the impressive double doors opened and an immaculately uniformed German officer appeared. He returned the major's salute in a casual manner, then halted at the top of the steps, one hand on hip, staring coldly down at us with pale eyes.

'What do you want?' he asked.

'Tell the colonel that I have the means to blow this building apart within minutes unless he decides to spare the lives of his men and surrender at once. Tell him that the invasion has succeeded, the town is surrounded and there is no escape,' said Major Tunstall.

I translated. The German seemed amused.

'Do you take us for fools?' he said. 'Your raid, while impressive, is merely intended to distract our attention from the Pas-de-Calais, where the real invasion will come.

That is the conclusion of our High Command. Soon you will be driven back to your ships, as you were at Dieppe, and I shall be asking for *your* surrender!'

I translated.

'Ask him if that is his last word on the subject,' said Major Tunstall.

'Not quite,' replied the German with a superior smile. 'You may tell your major that I was at Dunkirk, so he is not the first British officer I have seen with a white flag!'

'Please convey my compliments to the colonel,' responded Major Tunstall drily, 'and inform him that since he has chosen to ignore my advice, the chances of his ever seeing another British officer are extremely remote!'

The German was clearly furious at having his taunt flung back in his face.

'You have one minute to get out of the square!' he bellowed. 'After that I shall order my men to resume firing!'

We hurried back across the cobbles.

'He seems to have some funny ideas, sir,' I said. 'What was all that about a raid, and why did he mention the Pas-de-Calais?'

The major chuckled.

'They've got it into their heads that we'll invade in the Calais area because it offers the shortest sea crossing,' he said. 'By landing in Normandy we've sold them the biggest dummy in history!'

I climbed back aboard the AVRE and started the engine. Beside me, Gloomy had already loaded the petard and was sitting with a second bomb on his lap while he peered through the machine-gun sight. I heard the major's voice on the wireless net.

'All stations Delta, move now. You know what to do. Out!'

'Driver, advance,' said Ron.

I let in the clutch and we began moving forward. As we entered the square we immediately came under fire from the town hall. Gloomy and Mike returned it until I swung hard left. I crossed the square, then neutral-turned to the right until we were bows-on to the enemy. Behind me, the other AVREs did likewise until we formed a line.

'All stations Delta. From the right, at two-second intervals, commence firing. Out.'

'Clever stuff,' said George. 'That's the way we bring down a cliff – we stagger the explosions so that the continuous vibrations break it apart.'

Through the visor I watched the bombs explode in succession. We were last in line and by the time we fired the building was already a ruin. Chimneys collapsed, the roof caved in, floors gave way, tiles rained down and even inside the vehicle we could hear the thunder of falling masonry.

By the time the second salvo had done its work, little remained of the town hall above first-floor level. The scene was clouded by thick dust rising from the still-falling debris. The Canadian infantry, bayonets fixed, charged past to take possession. I watched as a few shaken survivors, their hands raised in surrender, emerged from the rubble; the colonel I had spoken to was not among them.

'Thanks a lot!' shouted the officer commanding the infantry to the major. 'We owe you one.'

As we drove out of the square I saw that the Canadian engineers were already at work clearing the road-blocks.

I had lost track of time and was surprised that dusk was closing in when we returned to the rally point. We all had maintenance and replenishment tasks to complete before we could turn in for what remained of the short midsummer night. I think we were too keyed up to sleep, so after we had made ourselves a brew of tea and a meal from our compo rations, we just sat round the petrol cooker, talking quietly until we dozed off.

It had been our first day's fighting together, an incredible, momentous day. We were all surprised at just how versatile the AVRE had proved to be, and we were pleased that we had saved so many Allied lives. There was also the thought that, having broken the Atlantic Wall, we had served our purpose. I wondered what the future might hold for us now.

Chapter 9
Firestorm

As things turned out, after the first day, we weren't required to do much at all during the next few weeks. And I learned the truth of the saying that war is 10 per cent sheer terror and 90 per cent boredom. It was true that we had taken the enemy completely by surprise by launching the invasion in Normandy rather than in the Calais area, but the problem was that inland the countryside consisted of small fields separated by steep earth banks topped with hedges. This sort of ground provided the Germans with ideal defensive positions because it made the going so difficult for tanks. The enemy were stubborn fighters anyway, so our beachhead expanded very slowly. Naturally, we got fed up with being stuck in one place with the battle raging only a few miles away. When newspapers arrived from England, we were all interested to read of our own exploits.

'It says here that the D-Day landings were such a success because the troops leading the beach assault were equipped with secret weapons,' said Mike, who had turned a pile of jerricans into an armchair.

'Aye, that's gottae be us,' commented Jock. 'Take a bow, fellers, ye're doin' great!'

Most of our time was spent making the beaches safe by clearing minefields and the wreckage of the German defences. Occasionally an assault team would be dispatched inland for a specific task, such as clearing a fortified village or putting in an SBG bridge to create a river crossing. The division seemed to function just like the company I had worked for at home. When an operation was planned, a representative would visit the site and decide what was needed. Then the right number of Crabs and AVREs would be sent to do the job with the appropriate equipment, returning to divisional control as soon as it had been completed.

Early in July, Mr Francis called us together. I could see from his expression that he was worried and guessed that we were in for an unusual mission.

'As you know,' he said, 'the Americans have captured Cherbourg. However, a nearby coast-defence battery remains in enemy hands and is making a great nuisance of itself by shelling all shipping approaching the American beachhead.'

'Yes,' said Gloomy unexpectedly, bringing the briefing to a sudden halt.

'What d'you mean, "yes"?' snarled Ron. 'What do you know about it?'

Gloomy shook his head sadly. 'Well, something always goes wrong, doesn't it, sarge?'

Ron glared at him ferociously.

'Someone tell me he doesn't exist! Tell me I've had too much sun and he's not real!'

'Och, he's real enough, sarge!' said Jock. 'Ah've seen him in the vehicle sometimes, but ah've no idea what he gets up to!'

'Let's get on, shall we?' said Mr Francis sharply.

We stopped laughing and pulled ourselves together.

'The battery is called Fort Chambray and is located on the tip of a peninsula,' continued the troop leader. 'The approaches to it are covered by an anti-tank ditch, a minefield and a number of reinforced-concrete bunkers containing anti-tank guns and machine-guns. The fort itself has masonry walls and is surrounded by a dry moat. The coast-defence guns are in the cliff face beneath the fort and are almost impossible to get at by normal methods. The Americans have no armoured assault engineer vehicles of their own, so they've asked for our help.'

There was a worried murmur among the crews. Despite the success we'd had when we first arrived, this mission sounded unbelievably difficult.

'Our own troop has been selected,' continued Mr Francis. 'Equipment will include two fascines, an SBG bridge and a Goat demolition frame. We'll also have an Ark attached to us.'

I had come across the Ark before. It was simply a turretless Churchill with folding ramps fitted to the top of the hull. After it had been driven into an anti-tank ditch, the ramps were folded down at either end and other vehicles used it as a bridge.

'As usual, we'll be working with a troop of Crabs from the South Galloway Horse. Also present will be some new arrivals in Normandy. The equipment they have is deadly and is still classified as top secret. Prepare to move in two hours' time.'

Only a madman enjoys going into battle, but I was glad to be on the move again because even our small contribution would help shorten the war. Speed was important, but in view of the distance involved we travelled overnight on tank transporters to save wear and tear on our own vehicles. We reached the assembly area the following morning to find that everyone else had already arrived. Among them were what appeared to be three conventional Churchill gun tanks towing strange armoured trailers. I walked over to look at them.

'Does the trailer give you extra fuel capacity?' I asked one of the drivers.

He shook his head. 'This is the Crocodile flame-thrower,' he said. 'The trailer holds fuel for the flame gun here.'

He pointed to the front of the tank where the hull machine-gun had been replaced by a nozzle incorporating what looked like a big spark plug.

'The projector will throw a thick jet of flame over 90 yards, using long or short bursts,' he said. 'Stay away from it – it will stick to you like glue until it burns itself out.'

I tried to imagine what it must be like to be on the receiving end. The thought horrified me. It must have shown in my expression.

'I know, it's inhuman,' said the driver. 'After we've used them once or twice, we hope just the appearance of Crocodiles will persuade the enemy to surrender. That way we save lives on both sides, especially our own blokes.'

It wasn't a job I'd have chosen for myself, but I could see that someone had to do it. Later that day the Crocodiles gave us a short demonstration and the results were even more terrible than I'd imagined. They turned a piece of gorse-covered ground into a blackened, smoking waste in which nothing survived.

The Americans were glad to see us. They were as fed up with chicken as we were with corned beef and I arranged to swap several tins of each, as well as some books and comics. They took us to see the ground over which we would be operating next day. In the distance, on the highest point of the headland, I could see the fort, with a track leading up to its ornamental gateway. Halfway down the slope were two large concrete bunkers, sunk deep into the earth. There were also a number of smaller bunkers covering the anti-tank ditch stretching across the neck of the peninsula. Three or four fire-blackened Shermans lay along the edge of the ditch.

That evening, the Americans briefed us on

the attack, which would be in two phases. The first would involve neutralizing the bunkers; the second, breaking into the fort. Afterwards, over dinner, I heard Mike discussing our part in detail with Ron. He had recently become interested in tactics, perhaps because the logic of the subject appealed to his surveyor's mind. I wondered if the more responsible side of him was beginning to show at last. Ron's thoughts were evidently similar because he spoke to him like an older brother.

'You're wasting your time here,' he said. 'You know what I'm talking about, don't you?'

'You mean I should apply for a commission? I've already said: I just don't want the responsibility for men getting killed or injured.'

'So you'll leave it to other people, will you? People like Major Tunstall, Mr Francis and me? Why should we give you a free ride when you've the brains and the ability?'

'Aye, well, he's a guid gunner, sarge! Ye'll no deny that?' said Jock, springing to Mike's defence.

'I can get a another petard gunner when I need one,' snapped Ron. 'It's trained, intelligent, experienced officers the Army needs.'

'Ron's right,' I said. 'I was hoping you were having second thoughts about this.'

We had never put Mike under such pressure before. He sat staring thoughtfully at the flames from the petrol cooker for a while.

'Maybe,' he said. 'I'll think about it when this is over.'

His attitude annoyed me. Situations could arise when I would be responsible for the rest of the crew. I didn't like it, but accepted the risk and hoped I would make the right decisions when the time came. I felt Mike was letting us down, but I knew the decision had to be his.

Phase one began at first light. It was misty and through the visor I could see that the Americans were firing smoke shells to try and mask our movements. Our first task was to create crossings over the anti-tank ditch to the right of the track. This would be done with the Ark and two fascines, one carried by ourselves and the other by Mr Francis's AVRE. Because visibility was so limited, Ron was commanding our vehicle from the top of the fascine, using an extension lead from his headset to the intercom.

'Can't say I'm enjoying this,' said his voice in my earphones. 'The other side is firing into the smoke. They can't see anything, but there are rounds hitting the bundle and cracking past my head too close for comfort.'

We had measured how far we had to go on the map and I was checking our progress very carefully on the mileometer. When I knew that the ditch lay just ahead I attracted Ron's attention by pressing the driver's buzzer twice as agreed.

'Dead slow,' said Ron. 'There it is – 20 yards ahead. Creep up to the edge and halt.'

I followed Ron's instructions. Behind me I heard him dropping into the turret from his precarious perch.

'It's free,' he said as he pulled the fascine release. 'Give her a nudge.'

I jerked the vehicle forward sharply. I felt the fascine rock, but nothing happened.

'And again – give it some welly this time!'

I knew I was dangerously close to the edge of the ditch, but it had to be done. I increased the revs and let in the clutch sharply. The AVRE lurched forward. I braked hard and the huge bundle toppled forward down the front of the vehicle. I felt the suspension springs ease as they were freed from its weight.

'Well done,' said Ron. 'Nice position, too. Reverse!'

We moved out of the way to let the three

Crabs across. I opened the sponson door to look around. I could see the four-man crew of the Ark. Having driven into the ditch, they were opening the flaps at either end of their vehicle. Beyond, I could see Mr Francis's AVRE had dropped its fascine and was reversing away. The Crabs came past and began flailing as soon as they had crossed the ditch. We waited nervously until their commander reported that they had cleared three lanes through the minefield, which was not as extensive as we had thought. I watched the American infantry and Shermans go over to clear the minor bunkers. From the fog ahead came the sound of explosions and fighting. I couldn't see, but I knew the tanks would be eliminating the enemy's machine-gun posts while the infantry dealt with his anti-tank guns. Casualties began to trickle back and in places the red glow of fires appeared in the mist.

After an hour the smoke thinned and the sun began to burn off the mist. Two of the Shermans and a Crab were burning, but the rest of the tanks were engaging the massive bunker up the hill that was our objective.

'All stations Delta Two, move now. Out!' said Mr Francis.

I was relieved to get moving again. The three AVREs in our troop advanced up the cleared lanes in the minefield. I could see the round helmets of the American infantry, pinned down in folds across the ground, several hundred yards short of the objective. We passed through them and continued uphill.

'Halt!' said Ron.

We were now within petard range of the bunker. I could see fire spitting out of the slits and saw a flash in one of them. There was crash from behind and above.

'Fire, for Pete's sake!' shouted Ron. 'What are you waiting for?'

Mike had already pressed the trigger and the bomb was on its way, bursting against the offending slit. Bombs from the other vehicles followed, smashing great chunks off the concrete. Gloomy alternately loaded the petard and kept his machine-gun firing as the bombardment continued.

I felt the vehicle shudder.

'What's happened?' I asked. 'Have we been hit?'

'Aye,' said Jock's voice on the intercom. 'The mushroom ventilator's been shot off the turret roof.'

We had been a sitting duck, but the

covering fire from the Crabs and Shermans must have upset the anti-tank gunner's aim, and I was very grateful. However, our bombardment didn't seem to be having much effect, because I could still see machine-gun fire flickering in many of the slits.

'Cease firing!' said Ron suddenly. 'Our new friends will take over for a while.'

The Crocodiles had moved up into the gaps between our AVREs. Great rods of flame reached out, splashing and blazing over the entire surface of the bunker. I realized that in addition to the fearful burning, the flame must be consuming the enemy's oxygen supply.

'How can they breathe in there?' I said aloud.

It seemed that they could, because seconds after the flaming had ended the enemy fire slits came to life again.

'Something's wrong,' said Ron in a puzzled voice. 'They may be sheltering behind blast walls in there, or have run up the exit tunnel until the flaming stopped. Even so, the petards should have cracked open the roof and allowed the flame to drop down inside.'

'It must be the concrete,' I said. 'It's too thick. I think I have an idea though. Why don't we all concentrate our petard fire against the corner of one of the slits? It's a weak point and if we start a crack we can go on enlarging it until the flame penetrates.'

'Yes, that might just do the trick,' said Ron. 'I'll put it to the troop leader.'

Mr Francis agreed and we took as our point of aim the fire slit of the anti-tank gun. After three shots a small crack began to spread upwards from the top left-hand corner. We concentrated on that until it grew wider and finally spread across the roof.

'All stations Delta Two, cease firing!' said Mr Francis. 'Our friends are going to have another go. Out.'

Once again the flame rods reached out, drenching the bunker under an inferno of red fire and black, oily smoke. Half a minute later more black smoke began to emerge from the fire slits. Then, waving a white flag, a crowd of Germans appeared from a concealed entrance beyond the bunker. They were carrying several badly injured comrades with them. The American infantry went forward to round them up.

After that we managed to complete phase one of the operation very quickly. It was a good job, because Gloomy said we were running low on Flying Dustbins. The AVREs, Crocodiles and gun tanks crossed the track to tackle the remaining bunker, but its occupants, having seen what had happened to their comrades, were in no mood for a fight and came out to surrender even before we were within range.

We had, we felt, done a satisfactory morning's work. While the Americans consolidated their positions on the newly won ground, we retired across the anti-tank ditch to prepare for phase two, which, for us assault engineers, promised to be even more testing, difficult and dangerous. None of us had tackled this sort of job before and what lay inside the blank walls of the fort was a mystery.

Chapter 10

The Goat and the Crocodile

Back at our harbour area, we set to replenishing our fuel and ammunition as well as fitting an SBG bridge to Mr Francis's AVRE and a Goat demolition frame to our own. Our third AVRE, commanded by Sergeant Jim Bassett, would accompany us to provide moral support and give covering fire as necessary. Near by, the Crocodile crews were refilling their trailers with flame fluid and the nitrogen gas cylinders that provided the propellant. We were unsure what to expect as we smashed our way into the fort, and so were relieved when an American engineer colonel arrived with a complete set of plans.

'Got them from a contractor in the village,' he said triumphantly. 'Used to do a lot of maintenance up there when the French Army had the place.'

We gathered round while he and Mr Francis examined the plans.

'See here, there's a short wooden drawbridge over the dry moat,' said the colonel. 'At the moment it's raised, but I'll fix it so our gun tanks smash it up before you arrive, just so it won't be in your way. Your SBG bridge is plenty long enough to span the gap and the contractor confirms there's a good wide ledge on the other side, in front of the gates.'

'What about the gates, colonel?' asked Mr Francis. 'I've got them down as being covered in sheet steel.'

'Yep, that's what he says, too.'

'Why can't we just blow them in with the petard, sir?' I said. 'It would be quicker than using the Goat.'

'Because we think there's a portcullis right behind them,' replied the troop leader.

'A what?' asked Jock.

'It's a steel grille lowered by winch from a room above, and it runs in grooves cut into the walls on either side,' explained Mr Francis. 'If we just blow in the gates, then we're not much better off, but by using a much larger charge we can blow in the gates *and* bulge the portcullis inwards enough to force it out of the grooves. Then we'll be able to bomb or ram our way through the wreckage into the interior. Is there anything you want to add, colonel?'

'Nope, I guess you got it figured about right, son. The portcullis is a pretty old-fashioned thing, but it's useful and what you'd expect to find in a place built centuries ago. The Frenchman says it's still there, so you're correct to assume the enemy will use it. Just one more thing . . .' His finger travelled into the interior of the fort, coming to rest in a corner. 'These here are steel blast doors. You'll find them locked. Behind them are steps leading down to the gun position.'

'What kind of opposition can we expect, sir?' asked Mike.

'Well, since you squashed those bunkers this morning, they don't have much to offer. There'll be plenty of small arms and machine-gun fire, of course, maybe some mortars and perhaps the odd guy with a bazooka. We'll do everything we can to keep them off your back.'

Despite our attack the previous day, the German coast-defence guns had been firing slowly but steadily for most of the day, their smoke sometimes blowing back over the edge of the cliff.

'How soon can you move, l'tenant?' asked

the American. We all knew what was on his mind.

'I've agreed with the Crocodile troop that we'll move off in ten minutes, sir.'

'OK – the sooner those guns are silenced the better. I don't want any more of our boys getting killed than we can possibly help. I'll go tell the rest of the guys what's needed.'

'Message from the Crabs, sir,' Jock shouted from the turret. 'They say the track leading up to the fort is clear o' mines.'

'Right, then,' said Mr Francis, 'the Crocodiles seem about ready, so let's mount up and get on our way.'

He led with the SBG, followed by Sergeant Bassett's AVRE, which was to shield our Goat from the worst effects of the enemy fire. I didn't like carrying the Goat. I was worried that if it was hit it would blow up and take the front of the AVRE with it. I knew I was being illogical because the electrically fired charges were all shaped to blow outwards, but the fear was real enough and I drove as close to the rear of Bassett's vehicle as I could. The real danger from enemy fire was that it would damage the wiring circuit.

I drove over the anti-tank ditch and began to climb. As we came level with the charred ruin of the bunker I could see some of the Shermans blasting away at the raised drawbridge with high explosive. Timber decking and girders flew off it until the last of the wreckage collapsed into the dry moat. More tanks were engaging the fire slits in the fort's casemates, but I was still conscious of enemy rounds striking our armour.

'All stations Delta Two, I'm going in!' said Mr Francis over the net. 'Delta Two-Able, stand by – Delta Two, out.'

I watched his AVRE nose slowly on to the drawbridge approach. Suddenly the SBG rigging went slack and I knew the bridge was down. I could hear the relief in the troop leader's voice as his vehicle reversed out of the way.

'Delta Two, it's a good, firm lie. Come on, Delta Two-Able, it's your turn now! Out.'

'That's us,' said Ron. 'Off you go, John, and take the last few yards at a crawl.'

I drove slowly across the SGB and halted just feet from the great, steel-covered double doors, which were already pitted with shot. I watched the mechanical arms lower the Goat frame until it was vertical.

'Take us forward another foot, will you, John?'

It was George Meade, our demolition NCO,

who was personally responsible for this phase of the operation. I inched forward until pressure on the arms told me that the Goat was in contact with the doors.

'That should do it,' said George. 'Stand by. Firing – now!'

Nothing happened.

'Check your switches!' I heard Ron say.

'Stand by. Firing – now!'

Again, nothing happened.

'The fault's outside,' said George. 'I'll have to check over the frame.'

He wriggled out of the sponson door. Knowing how slow and meticulous he was, I gave Gloomy a nudge.

'Come on, let's give him a hand.'

We found ourselves beneath an arch. George was humming to himself as he checked the wires to each of the charges. We followed his example and began checking the rest. There was a clatter as something bounced off the AVRE and exploded in the moat below. More explosions followed. We were concealed from the Germans on the wall above the gate by the arch, but they were tossing stick grenades at us.

It wasn't pleasant and I thought it would only be a matter of time before one or more of us was hit. Granite chippings rained down on us as our two supporting AVREs opened up with their machine-guns. The grenading stopped. Some 50 yards on either side of us two of the Crocodiles had begun flaming the casemates. The heat was terrific and the oily stench turned my stomach.

'Ah, here's the problem,' said George, indicating two faulty connections. We fixed them and scrambled back aboard.

'Stand by,' said George. 'Firing – now!'

Nothing happened. As we went out again I could see that George was close to despair. He had done everything possible, yet still the Goat refused to fire. We checked connections again and found nothing out of place. I began examining the main lead back to the AVRE, running my fingers along it inch by inch. At one point I felt a roughness and saw that it had been nicked. When I opened the insulation, several torn strands of copper wire were revealed.

'Got it!' I said. 'It looks as though it's been cut by a bullet.'

'Good lad!' said George approvingly. 'Well, we'll soon have that fixed.'

It took only minutes, although it seemed like hours as he exposed the broken wires, carefully rejoined them and bound them with tape, humming all the time.

'Right!' he said. 'Let's have another go, shall we?'

Once more, we clambered aboard.

'Stand by! Firing – now!'

There was a thunderclap explosion. The huge doors were hurled inwards off their hinges, seemed to hang for a second and then collapsed in a cloud of dust and smoke.

'Nice one, Mr Bang!' said Jock. 'That's one o' ye're best yet!'

When the smoke cleared I could see that the doors were lying on top of the portcullis, one side of which had been torn out of its groove. Half the other side was still in place, leaving the twisted grille at an angle, with the doors lying on top. Beyond, I could see figures running in the fort's courtyard and several shots came our way.

'Reckon you can get us over that?' asked Ron.

'Yes, I think so,' I replied. 'The weight of the vehicle should bring down the rest of that ironwork.'

'Off you go, then. Mike, Gloomy, give 'em all you've got!'

I let in the clutch, increasing power to the engine. Slowly, the AVRE began climbing the ramp created by the fallen doors. There was the sound of twisting, tearing metal as the portcullis was ripped free. The pile of debris collapsed beneath us but I kept going. Beside me, Gloomy was hammering away with his machine-gun. The confined space of the gateway tunnel magnified the sound many times. As we emerged, we came under heavy fire from several directions. Mike let fly with the petard, bringing down part of a barrack block opposite. Ron shouted a warning.

'*Gloomy – don't reload!* You'll get your miserable head blown off!'

We cruised round the courtyard, machine-gunning for all we were worth.

'Where's everyone else?' I shouted.

A man with a panzerfaust, the German equivalent of the bazooka, darted out of a doorway ahead of us. He took hasty aim, fired, and disappeared quickly. The bomb exploded against the starboard air intake. It did not penetrate the main armour, but the blast caused the engine to cut out. It took a full minute for me to restart it and still no other AVREs had arrived.

'Without support we've got no chance,' Gloomy yelled above the noise.

In that second, a horrible, icy thought shot through my mind – this is where you're going to die!

Chapter 11

Vengeance from the Skies

At that moment a Crocodile, belching flame, emerged from the gateway arch, followed by some American infantrymen and the rest of our troop.

'Thank God,' I whispered, fully realizing that I had barely escaped death.

The Germans must have known they were outgunned and gave up, appearing from all sorts of nooks and crannies with their hands raised. However, I noticed that even while the prisoners were being marched off, the big guns beneath the fort continued to fire. I could see that the Crocodile's commander, Mr Francis and an American major were interrogating a senior German officer. As I got out to stretch my legs, Mr Francis beckoned me.

'This officer apparently does not understand what we require him to do,' he said, pointing to the steel blast doors in the corner of the courtyard. 'He is to order his men in the battery below to cease firing and surrender immediately.'

I translated, but the German merely shrugged.

'It is the duty of those men to fight on as long as possible,' he said. 'I shall not order them to do otherwise.'

The eyes of the American major were cold and hard.

'OK, corporal,' he said to me, 'tell him he's got two minutes to give the order or you guys will blow in his fancy tin doors and blowtorch everything inside!'

I explained what would happen.

'You saw how easily we smashed in your gates, and you've seen what the flame-throwers can do. Do you want your men to die a horrible death?'

The prospect horrified me, too, but we were dealing with an enemy we knew to be ruthless, so this was something he would understand.

The German did not reply. Instead, he walked over to the blast doors, opened a recessed hatch and spoke into a telephone. After a minute or so the doors opened and the gun crews came up the steps, emerging into the courtyard with their hands raised.

They were quickly bundled into line and disappeared through the gate.

'Good job,' said Mr Francis, turning to the rest of the crew. 'I think you boys deserve a well-earned rest. Return to base, the infantry can handle things here.'

I was relieved to leave the fort. It had been too close a call for my liking.

That evening we were enjoying a meal and a brew when a convoy of Jeeps drew up. A number of senior American officers stepped out, including the engineer colonel, the colonel commanding the infantry regiment that had carried out the assault with us, and no less a person than the major-general commanding the division. I watched as they went round the entire British battlegroup, from the Crabs to the Crocodiles, and then to us. Mr Francis was about to call us up to attention when the general waved us to sit down again.

'At ease, men!' he said. 'You boys get right on with your chow, because you've earned it. This is kinda informal, but I want to thank you for what you did up there. You were a credit to your Army and your corps and, most of all, you've saved a lot of American lives. Uncle Sam is grateful and, believe me, he doesn't forget!'

After the general had gone, we sat basking in the glow of his words for a while. Ron broke the silence.

'He was right. It was a good effort – well done, all of you.'

'Aye, well, what d'ye expect?' said Jock. 'We're just invincible, that's a'!'

'That's it!' exclaimed Ron. 'We'll call her *Invincible*!'

Major Tunstall had been at us for some time to give our AVRE a name, but we hadn't been able to agree. This time there was no argument, and *Invincible* it was.

The Americans were as good as their word. They asked Mr Francis for his recommendations and, shortly after we had returned to our own sector, several members of the troop, including George Meade, Gloomy and me, were ordered to report to 79th Armoured Division Headquarters. There, in the presence of Major-General Hobart, a visiting American brigadier-general presented us with decorations which we were told were the equivalent of our Military Medal. We were pleased, of course, but a little surprised. After all, we had only been doing our jobs.

Major-General Hobart was obviously pleased as well, because he shook our hands and congratulated us each in turn. When he reached Gloomy a glimmer of alarmed recognition crossed his face.

'I've seen you somewhere before, haven't I?'

'Yes, sir. I told you we'd flatten Hitler's Atlantic Wall and we have, haven't we?'

'Quite so – well done,' said the general, and hurriedly passed on.

A couple of days later I was ordered to report to Major Tunstall.

'You have proved to be a capable NCO, Corporal Smith, so I am rewarding you with a second stripe,' he said.

'Thank you, sir,' I replied.

'That, however, is not why I want to talk to you,' he continued. 'Twice now your knowledge of German has proved invaluable to us. In the circumstances, it is only fair to tell you that your promotion prospects would be even better if you were to transfer to the Intelligence Corps. Do you wish me to arrange a transfer, or do you prefer to remain with us?'

The choice lay between a sergeant's stripes, better pay and living conditions on the one hand, and staying with the lads on the other. It took me just one second to reach a decision.

'I'll stay, sir.'

'Good. I'm glad,' said the major, and that was that.

This time there were no reservations about my promotion.

'Ye're headin' for stardom, just like me!' said Jock. 'I'll lend ye a pair o' dark glasses so ye can go out in public without bein' recognized!'

'Yes, well done,' said Mike. 'You deserve it.'

The heavy fighting to expand the beachhead continued day after day. As usual, our division contributed assault teams to various operations, but we weren't involved because *Invincible* needed some heavy repairs and was in the hands of the fitters. This gave me a chance to catch up on my mail, a bundle of which was waiting for me when we got back from the American sector. I settled down to read the letters in date order.

The newspapers had said that the enemy had started a new blitz against south-eastern England, using something called a flying bomb. This was apparently a sort of pilotless aircraft, the nose of which was packed with high explosive. It was driven by a rocket motor and when the fuel ran out it dived straight into the ground, where it blew up. If one fell on a built-up area it could cause serious damage and heavy loss of life. My parents said very little about them because they obviously did not want to worry me.

There was also a small parcel containing a letter from Great-aunt Lavinia, in which she also referred to the flying bombs:

The kaiser has been sending over his newest aeroplanes. People say they don't have pilots. How stupid! Of course, they don't know where to go, and crash wherever they like, damaging a lot of private property. Maude Dickinson was so shaken by one explosion that she has completely mislaid her knitting. Kindly inform your officers that I expect them to do something about this.

Now you're in France I want you to visit Paris very shortly. Look up the Comte de Marsin, a charming man who paid me many extravagant compliments. He will probably invite you to his château.

I'm enclosing some snuff I found in your great uncle's study. He always said it was a great comfort when the Boxer rebels besieged him in the Peking legation.

I chuckled at the thought of Mr Francis, Captain Holroyd and Major Tunstall looking for Maude Dickinson's knitting, although of course I knew she was referring to the flying bombs. The count, if he was still alive, would be a very ancient person – and there was the small matter of half the German Army blocking my way to Paris. As for her present, I had no intention of sticking any sort of snuff up my nose, let alone Chinese snuff over forty years old! Unfortunately, I left it lying about. Gloomy, whose turn it was to cook for the crew that day, thought it was curry powder and put it in the stew. He nearly killed the lot of us!

A few days later we had another delivery of mail. My parents told me that a flying bomb had destroyed the house behind ours, killing everyone inside. I was sorry to hear this because they were a nice family, and I seriously worried about the danger my own folks were in.

'Bad news, corp?' said Gloomy, looking up from his own pile of letters.

I nodded.

'My folks are all right, but their neighbours have been killed by a flying bomb. How are things at your end of town?'

'Not good,' he said. 'I'm going to try and put it to the back of my mind. We can't do anything about it, so worrying won't do us any good. It's hard, but that's the way the folks at home think about us.'

That was one of the remarkable things about Gloomy: when things were really bad he stopped complaining and displayed a lot of tough, practical common sense. The flying bombs were causing concern at every level. The following morning Major Tunstall called the squadron together informally.

'These things are what Hitler calls his Vengeance Weapons,' he said. 'They are intended to undermine civilian morale at home so that our government will open peace negotiations. It won't, of course, but there's no telling what a madman like that will think. Fortunately, they have a very limited range, although that is no comfort to those of us whose families live in London or south-eastern England. The launching sites are in the Pas-de-Calais and on the Belgian coast. I can tell you that once we break out of this beachhead, one of the Army commander's top priorities is to eliminate them.'

'Why can't the RAF bomb them, sir?' I asked.

'Good point. It's been tried, but with very limited success. The problem is that they consist of little more than launching ramps which are widely dispersed and easy to conceal from the air. We have, however, found ways in which the flying bombs can be dealt with. They are fast, but the latest Spitfires can catch them and shoot them down; not only that, by flying alongside them the Spitfires can flip their wings over so that they dive into the Channel. Furthermore, all of London's anti-aircraft guns have been moved down to the Kent coast, so by no means all the bombs launched are getting through.'

There was a heavy silence, because we all knew that the damage was being caused by the bombs that did get through.

'I know what you're thinking, because I'm probably thinking the same thing,' said the major. 'Perhaps it will help if I tell you that the end of the campaign here in Normandy is a lot closer than it seems. After that, I believe that the pace of operations will be much faster, enabling us to put an end to this menace.'

We didn't need any further motivation. From that moment on I think all of us were driven by the need to break out of the beachhead and overrun the launching sites as quickly as possible.

We did not have long to wait. At the end of July we heard that the Americans had broken through the enemy front at the southern end of the Allied beachhead. At the same time, we knew that our own infantry and armoured divisions, plus those of the Canadians and the Poles, were fighting their way steadily south from Caen against tough opposition. By 16 August the German armies in Normandy had been surrounded near Falaise, and within a few days they had been completely destroyed.

In one way, I felt disappointed that I had not been involved in the battle, although during its final stages there had been little for the assault engineering teams to do. In any event, we had only just got *Invincible* back from the workshops and were still kitting her out when the fighting ended. The bustle in our harbour area and the serious expressions on the faces of the officers all suggested that the squadron would be going into action again very shortly.

'What's going on?' I asked Ron, who had been quiet and withdrawn for a couple of days.

'There aren't any details yet, but Mr Francis thinks we may be going to have a go at Le Havre,' he replied. 'It's heavily fortified and he says we're probably in for the biggest scrap since D-Day.'

For a moment I felt my stomach muscles tighten in the same way they had aboard the landing-craft. Could I face that sort of massive destruction again? But then I remembered that this would be one step towards the elimination of the flying-bomb sites. I couldn't do anything about the fear and the risks, but if the result helped bring safety to those at home I'd have to put up with them.

Chapter 12

Descent into Darkness

At the beginning of September we began trundling northwards along crowded roads in the wake of the Army's whirlwind advance across northern France towards the Belgian frontier. We crossed the River Seine by a pontoon bridge, but instead of continuing northwards our convoy swung west. The rumours had been right. We were to attack Le Havre, spearheading the assault of two British infantry divisions, the 49th (West Riding) and the 51st (Highland), two of the finest fighting divisions in the Army.

Before we moved off to join our assault teams, Major Tunstall called us together to explain why the operation was necessary.

'As you know,' he said, 'the Dieppe raid proved that it would be impossible for us to capture one of the Channel ports, and that is why we brought our own prefabricated Mulberry harbour with us when we invaded.

The situation has now changed. We are advancing at such a pace that the Mulberry cannot keep up with the Army's fuel requirements. We therefore need at least one of the Channel ports to ease the strain on the supply services.'

'I realize that, sir,' said Ron, 'but I don't understand why the Germans have decided to hold out here when they're retreating everywhere else.'

'The answer is simple,' replied the major. 'Mad as Hitler undoubtedly is, he understands our situation and has decided to deny us the ports. Deserters tell us that he has designated them fortresses and given orders for their garrisons to fight to the last man.'

'Do you think they will, sir?' asked Mike.

'As you'll have heard, on 20 July several of his generals tried to kill Hitler with a bomb. Some of them have already been executed and the rest are now too frightened to do anything except obey orders. My guess is that whoever is in command here will fight on until his engineers have wrecked the harbour, then surrender.'

To my mind, that meant that we would meet fanatical resistance, and I didn't like the idea. As we left the briefing and drove off to our forming-up areas, the mood was sombre. The assault teams consisted of Crabs, Crocodiles and AVREs with various devices, depending on what sort of opposition we expected to encounter. Le Havre's defences covered a wide area. The principal obstacle was an anti-tank ditch with a deep minefield on either side, covered by a series of interconnected strong points. Behind these lay the town, in which street-fighting could be expected.

It had rained heavily during the night, but Sunday 10 September dawned fine. The clouds were breaking up and I was hoping for a strong east wind which would dry out the heavy clay soil so that the well-laden AVREs could cross it without too much difficulty. The day developed into a beautiful sunlit afternoon.

I was sitting on *Invincible's* turret with the rest of the lads when the battle began at 1700 hours. For thirty minutes bombers flew over in a continuous stream until the defences seemed to vanish beneath the rain of exploding bombs. Our own artillery then joined in with a spectacular bombardment. At 1745 we dropped into our seats as the assault teams began moving forward, led by their Crabs. Considering the punishment they had received, it seemed incredible to me that the enemy returned such a heavy fire.

One of the strange things about that battle was the large numbers of friendly French civilians who came out to watch. There were whole families of them, with the girls in bright summer frocks. They obviously didn't realize the danger they would be in once the fighting started. They wandered around the tanks and the gun positions until we chased them off. But despite our warnings, they kept popping up all over the place, smiling, waving and getting in everyone's way.

The Crabs on our own sector were hindered by the muddy ground and suffered severely. Some simply bogged down or were immobilized by deeply buried mines that their flailing chains had failed to explode. They became stationary targets for the enemy anti-tank guns and soon several were burning. One by one, the lanes they were clearing became blocked. In planning its operations, however, the division always allowed a safety margin, and on this occasion we were responsible for it.

'Hallo, Delta Two Able, move now. Out!' said Mr Francis.

'Driver, advance. Keep it slow. I'll tell you when to stop,' said Ron.

We were pushing a device called a Snake. It consisted of sections of 4-inch iron tube filled with explosive. Joined together, these produced a total length of 400 feet. The front section had a specially shaped head that stopped it digging it into the ground, but unless the device was handled carefully it had a tendency to wander to the left or right.

As I nervously approached the minefield we became the target of the enemy's anti-tank gunners. They had no idea what we were up to and aimed at the vehicle. I felt the strikes of two or three armour-piercing shot, but we were not penetrated.

'Mike, Gloomy, see if you can spot the gun flashes – give 'em a good hiding!' said Ron.

They both began hammering away.

'Slowly now – halt! Over to you, George.'

The Snake was detonated from inside the vehicle and thus was George's responsibility. I could see the edge of the anti-tank ditch, a little over 100 yards away.

'Firing – now!' said George.

Because of our experience when we were attacking the fort with the Americans, I half expected nothing to happen. Instead, there was a huge explosion and a flash stretching into the distance, followed immediately by many lesser explosions. When the smoke cleared I saw that the explosion of the Snake had triggered every mine in its vicinity, blasting a path 20 feet wide right across the minefield.

'Mr Bang strikes again!' shouted Jock.

A Crab from the reserve troop came past, crossed the minefield and cleared a turning space at the edge of the ditch. Mr Francis, grinning broadly as he gave us the thumbs-up, passed us with the assault team's SBG bridge, which he dropped neatly across the gap, then slotted into the turning space. The rest of the Crab troop followed. Beyond the ditch the ground sloped gently upwards to a plateau which was well drained, so the flails made better progress. Once lanes had been cleared, we were joined by the Crocodiles and set about eliminating the strong points one by one, using a combination of petard fire, flame and aggressive infantry attacks. After about a quarter of an hour, the defenders either surrendered or made a run for it.

My visor provided only limited vision at the best of times, and that was mainly straight ahead because the track horns were so far forward. I couldn't see much of the infantry, although I knew they were always there. We were approaching a piece of open woodland that we thought was clear of the enemy. Suddenly a man popped up from nowhere, just 30 yards ahead, and levelled a panzerfaust straight at us. I froze. I knew that he couldn't possibly miss. Time seemed to stand still as I waited for the blast.

Just as he pulled the trigger, he was bowled over backwards. The rocket shot upwards, to explode against a tree.

'Jeez – that was a close one!' I gasped as a hard-looking section of men from the King's Own Yorkshire Light Infantry ran past, bayonets levelled.

'Thanks a lot, lads!' I heard Ron shout from the turret. The section leader gave us a cheerful wave. If his blokes hadn't shot the panzerfaust man at once, we would all be dead or at best seriously injured. Another close escape.

We were approaching the highest point of the plateau. Sergeant Bassett broke into the net, his voice frantic.

'Delta Two Baker, Contact! Eighty-Eight on the crest dead ahead! He's –'

There was a big muzzle flash to my right front and the transmission ended.

'John, put your foot down if you want to live!'

Ron's voice sounded desperate. Only too aware that our lives depended on it, I gave *Invincible* all the power I could shove into her engine, but speed wasn't her strong point.

I knew the German 88 mm anti-tank gun was the best in the world. It could put an armour-piercing round right through the Churchill's thick armour without the slightest difficulty. The enemy's second shot had flashed past the rear of our turret, just above the engine deck. We reached the crest and were now level with the gun.

'Keep going!' shouted Ron. 'They've brewed up Bassett and his fascine is burning. Can't see how many of them got out.'

I kept going, taking advantage of the slope, which was now in our favour.

'Hard right!'

I turned the tiller bar and changed down.

'On!' I straightened up. We were now on course to pass behind the big 88. I could now see it, silhouetted against the flames of Sergeant Bassett's burning AVRE. It was dug in and the crew were struggling to swing it round towards us. One man was ready to load the big shell that would put an end to us.

'Mike, traverse right!' ordered Ron.

I sensed the turret turning behind and above me.

'On! You'll get one shot, so make it pay or it will be your last!'

We were now coming level with the gun, the barrel of which was still swinging slowly. It had become a deadly, slow-motion race with survival as the prize.

'Halt!'

Ron wanted to give Mike the best possible chance. I stamped on the brake and the AVRE rocked on its springs.

'FIRE!'

The bomb curved slowly through the air and exploded against the gun, scattering the crew in all directions.

For a while we just sat there and let the tension drain away. It was Jock who broke the silence.

'That's the last time a'm comin' out wi' you lot! Ye cannae stay out o' trouble!'

Mr Francis arrived.

'That was a close call,' he said. 'For a minute there I thought you were a goner.'

'How are Jim Bassett and his crew, sir?' asked Ron.

'Harrison and Jenkins are dead, I'm afraid, and Spencer has been badly wounded. Bassett and the rest got out with minor injuries and burns.'

We felt terribly saddened by this. The

troop had been together a long time and these were the worst casualties we had suffered, but we all understood that the battle had to continue.

'The problem for us,' said the troop leader, pointing to an area on the map where the plateau fell away into a narrow valley separating it from the town, 'is that Bassett was carrying the fascine we wanted to use here. There's a stream with steep banks in the bottom and we were going to use it to cross.'

His finger traced the stream until it was crossed by a track.

'We can try working round it. This looks promising, even if the track is closed by a road-block the other side.'

'It won't be easy, sir,' said Ron. 'The slope there is about 40 degrees and we'll be doing it in the dark. I don't like the look of it.'

We sat in a group while Mr Francis used the wireless to discuss his plan with the assault group commander.

'Well,' he said at length, 'it seems we're a bit ahead of our schedule. The infantry still have some mopping up to do, and while the Crocodiles agree that we'll have to divert, they're worried about their trailers on the slope. They're going to try about a mile further back, where it's not so steep, and join us at the bridge. By then I'm hoping we'll have knocked out the road-block.'

I could tell that Ron was uneasy about the idea.

'I suggest we drive over to the edge of the plateau and take a look, sir. That way we'll be able to see the slope and choose a route down if we think it's possible.'

We set off on a compass bearing, driving slowly over unknown terrain. From time to time the shadowy figures of Germans flitted across our front, evidently pulling back to new positions. They gave us no trouble and a burst or two from Gloomy's Besa machine-gun was usually enough to disperse them. We halted at the top of the slope we were to descend. Mr Francis disappeared into the gloom. I switched off the engine. In the silence I could hear the sounds of scattered fighting all round. From the direction of the harbour came the constant boom of demolitions.

After ten minutes the troop leader returned.

'I think I've found a way,' he said. 'I'll lead on foot. Follow me as closely as you can – it's a bit hairy in places but you can do it.'

I started up.

'You lot had better dismount,' I said into the intercom. 'I don't like this at all.'

Gloomy didn't move and there was no response from the turret. I engaged bottom gear and followed the light of Mr Francis's torch.

The vehicle tipped forward as we reached the edge. Very slowly, I started to descend, using the engine as a brake. It seemed to me that in places the slope was even steeper than 40 degrees. All sorts of terrifying thoughts raced through my mind. The soil was clay and probably still slippery beneath the surface. What if the AVRE behind lost control and smashed into us? My hands started to sweat. My own particular horror was crabbing. This happened when the vehicle got into an uncontrollable sideways slide on a slope like this. If the angle of descent increased or an obstacle was struck, the vehicle would overturn and career downwards. Even if the turret stayed on its ball race, the injuries sustained by those aboard would be horrific and someone would probably be killed.

I kept my eyes glued to the bouncing torchlight below. Suddenly, the rear end of the vehicle began breaking away slowly to the right. I applied a quick correction with the tiller bar, to no effect. My instinct was to brake, but I realized that this would only make matters worse. *Invincible* was starting to slide!

Chapter 13

A Matter of Honour

It took a real effort of will to press the accelerator down. I felt the tracks begin to bite as the extra power reached them, then I steered into the slide. We straightened up. I felt an enormous sense of relief.

There was a loud bang. I tensed, expecting the worst, but nothing seemed amiss and I carried on. There were two more bangs. The torch was telling me to swing right and halt. I did so, pulled on the handbrake and sat there, completely limp and soaked in sweat.

'Well done, John,' said Ron's voice. 'Nice piece of driving.'

'Och, don't go tellin' him that,' said Jock. 'He'll want more money!'

'I thought I told you lot to get out and walk!' I replied.

'What? And leave you in charge of an expensive piece of machinery like this?' said Ron.

I was touched and a little humbled by their confidence in me. The second AVRE completed its descent and pulled in behind.

'I suppose you know you've just walked through a minefield, sir?' shouted Ron to Mr Francis. 'Those bangs were Teller anti-personnel mines – they make a nasty mess of you if you brush against one of them.'

Horrified, Mr Francis just stood there gaping while we laughed.

'That'll teach you to take us mountaineering, sir!'

'Fair comment,' he said, rubbing his chin ruefully. 'I'll think twice about it next time.'

We were just 50 yards short of the bridge. No one seemed to be about, so George and Jock walked down the track to take a look. Five minutes later they were back with good news.

'It was wired for demolition, sir,' said George. 'I've cut the wires and removed the detonators for good measure. The enemy seems to have done a bunk.'

We drove up to the road-block beyond the bridge. That, too, was deserted. It wasn't much of an obstacle and George managed to clear it with a couple of small charges. There was still no sign of our infantry or the Crocodiles and we seemed to have lost wireless contact with both. I hoped it was because the plateau was screening our transmissions and nothing more serious. As it was so quiet, Mr Francis decided that he would drive back along the track and look for them.

Ron told me to pull on to the grass verge beyond the road-block. As I did so there was a heavy explosion beneath the vehicle, followed by a clattering noise as the shattered left-hand track ran off. Dust was shaken loose from every nook and cranny inside the vehicle, but there was no other apparent damage.

'Everyone all right?' said Ron. 'Anti-tank mine – mining the verges is an old German trick. I should have known better.'

We jumped out and began prodding the verge around the vehicle for anti-personnel and other mines. There didn't seem to be any more, but it would take some time to repair the track and replace a damaged bogie unit.

'George, Jock, come with me,' said Ron. 'We'll scout ahead a bit and cover the vehicle while the others are working.'

They disappeared into the pre-dawn gloom. Mike, Gloomy and I broke out the tools and set to. I began knocking out a track pin.

'John, we've got company,' said Gloomy in a low voice.

I looked up. The growing light revealed a pair of ornamental gates across the track. Beyond them a short drive led to an ornate villa. Standing at the gates was a man in a black beret and leather coat. He was carrying a Sten gun and had a brassard saying FFI on his right arm. He walked over to us and shook hands.

'Resistance?' I asked.

'Yes, *m'sieu*. My colleagues and I have a German general and his staff surrounded in the house. The general says he will surrender to the British but not to us, because he does not consider us to be soldiers. He says that if we attack, his men will resist and lives will be needlessly lost. Your arrival is most fortunate. Perhaps you can help?'

I didn't want to leave the AVRE unattended, so I told Mike and Gloomy to carry on while I took a look.

The Frenchman escorted me through the gates and up the drive. There were more Resistance fighters in the shrubbery and under cover at other points around the house. They seemed to be armed with everything from captured Schmeisser

140

machine-pistols to shotguns. Beside the front door was an official German Army plate inscribed *Festungsingenieur Le Havre*. So, that was who the general was – the fortress engineer for Le Havre. The door opened to reveal a German officer wearing the cords of an aide-de-camp.

'Follow me!' he snapped.

I followed him across the hall, where other staff officers and clerks, weapons in hand, were in position beside the windows. The aide knocked on a pair of double doors and I was shown inside. The general, a tall, distinguished-looking man in an immaculate uniform, was standing behind a highly polished table. The sight of me seemed to send him into a frenzy of rage.

'This is intolerable!' he shouted. 'You are not an officer! I shall only surrender to an officer! Get out and bring an officer to me immediately!'

'There's no need to shout, is there – sir?' I said evenly. 'You see, I'm neither deaf nor one of your soldiers. Still, I'll see if I can find anyone who can be bothered with you.'

His face went so red I thought he would burst a blood vessel.

We had no officer with us and I wasn't quite sure what to do, but as I reached the

AVRE a plan formed in my mind. I explained the situation to Mike and Gloomy.

'So what's your great idea?' asked Mike.

'It's simple really. You can pretend you're an officer and accept the general's surrender.'

'Have you gone mad?' he exclaimed. 'Do you know what the penalties are for impersonating an officer?'

'Death, I expect,' said Gloomy.

'Thanks, Gloomy, that's a great help,' I said. 'All you have to do, Mike, is let him think you are one. Apart from which, you want to be an actor, so think of it as a useful experience.'

'Well, since you put it like that,' he said. His manner changed abruptly. 'And you won't forget to salute me when we enter the general's office, will you, corporal?'

The transition was so real it gave me quite a start.

Back at the villa I opened the office door for Mike and threw him up my smartest salute. He strode briskly across to the general, who did not seem to have moved since I left him.

'I understand you wish to surrender, general,' said Mike in an uninterested tone. 'I'm rather busy, so can we conclude the formalities immediately?'

Meekly the general placed his pistol in Mike's outstretched hand.

'I have done my duty but I have no intention of dying for Adolf Hitler.'

'Have you wrecked the harbour?' asked Mike sharply.

'Yes. I have carried out my orders to the letter. It was a matter of honour.'

'Just as the Führer wanted,' said Mike contemptuously. 'I'll never understand you people. Tell your men to discard their weapons and walk out in single file with their hands up. My orderly will escort you to the gate.'

With that, he swept grandly out of the room. I felt like applauding.

When we reached the gate we found that the rest of the assault group had caught up. Our distinguished prisoner aroused much comment, but we were deliberately vague about how we had acquired him.

'Sorry about the orderly bit,' said Mike.

'Glad to have you back,' I replied. 'For a minute or two in there I didn't recognize you!'

'Look, I've been thinking,' he said after a moment. 'You took control then and sorted out a difficult situation. Maybe I've not been pulling my full weight so far.'

'Does that mean you've changed your mind about a commission?'

'Yes, I think so. I can't go on leaving everything to everyone else, can I? I'll apply when things quieten down again.'

'Good on you, Mike. I knew you'd come round in the end,' I said, giving him a friendly punch on the shoulder.

We had to wait until later in the morning for the fitters to arrive with a new bogie unit. Once we had this, we were able to complete the track repair quickly and then go forward to rejoin the battle. By now it was concentrated in the centre of Le Havre. Our AVRE wasn't heavily involved because so many civilians got in the way, and it took longer than it should have to eliminate the last pockets of resistance.

The squadron reassembled outside Le Havre after the battle. Major Tunstall, smiling broadly, came across and congratulated the troop on our part in it.

'You didn't know it,' he said, 'but the enemy thought that the hair-raising slope you came down was tank-proof. Your sudden appearance behind his lines upset him so badly that he abandoned a whole sector of the defences. Well done, everyone.'

We were all pleased with the success of the

battle, and so when the major called the squadron together later in the day I was puzzled by his serious expression.

'It's not good news, I'm afraid,' he said. 'Hitler has decided to employ a new weapon in his terror campaign. The flying bomb, now known as the V-1, has been joined by a more powerful rocket called the V-2. The V-2 is fired straight up into the stratosphere, and there is no defence against it. Nor is it possible to give a warning, because when its fuel runs out it drops straight to the ground. There is simply a massive explosion.'

I felt as though someone had flung a bucket of icy water over me. Things had been going so well, and now there was this new horror.

'Fortunately,' he continued, 'the Canadians have sealed off the Pas-de-Calais area, where the launching sites are located. They are now fighting their way into the defences, but in response to Hitler's direct order the enemy is offering fanatical resistance. We are therefore ordered to move north immediately and join the Canadians. I'm sure you're as glad of this as I am. We can put a stop to this once and for all.'

There was a murmur of approval. For me, and for Gloomy and many others, our next fight would be a very personal one. Despite feeling exhausted and confused from being pulled out of one battle and thrown straight into another, I was prepared for this one last fight. Except I hoped it wouldn't be my last.

Chapter 14

Turning the Tables

That evening, we loaded our AVREs and equipment on to tank transporters and began trundling north. When the assault on Calais began on 25 September, the assault teams, supported by naval gunfire and air attacks, functioned like well-oiled machinery. The Crabs flailed gaps in the minefields, then provided direct gunfire support for our AVREs as we bridged ditches and carried out demolitions. In turn, our petards cracked open bunkers which the Crocodiles flamed until the enemy gave in.

From time to time, behind the German lines, flaming discs rose high into the sky and vanished in the direction of England. They were, it seemed, determined to go on firing their V-2 rockets until the bitter end, and any one of them could kill our families and friends. Because of this we fought with a cold efficiency fuelled by anger.

By late afternoon we had taken the last of our designated objectives for the day. The Crocodiles and Crabs withdrew to their rally points but we were ordered to stay where we were and assist the infantry to capture a village. They were pinned down by fire from a terrace of large houses and wanted us to go in and eliminate the enemy stronghold. Ron brought us to within 50 yards of the gable end. Two Flying Dustbins brought part of it down, but Ron wasn't satisfied.

'Come on, Gloomy – reload!' he snapped.

'I can't – those were the last two,' said Gloomy.

'Want me to try ramming?' I asked.

'Yes – that should open it up nicely.'

As we approached the building at a slow but steady speed the enemy opened up with everything he had. The sound of rounds striking the armour was like metallic hail. Through the holes we had already made in the brickwork I could see alarmed figures scurrying about. As we struck the gable, more brickwork came tumbling down on top of us. I reversed. The hole didn't seem big enough, so I decided to go in again. I drove forward and smashed right through the outer wall into the interior of the house.

Suddenly, the bottom seemed to drop out

of the world. We were falling. As we landed with a crash my head cracked against the visor. I heard the thunder of bricks, beams and roof tiles falling on the vehicle, then I must have passed out briefly.

When I came to, the engine had stopped and there was a strong smell of petrol.

'Get out of there!' shouted a harsh voice outside. 'If you do not I shall set fire to the petrol and you will be burned alive!'

The turret hatches were jammed by fallen beams, but I managed to wriggle out of my sponson door. The rest of the crew followed me. Ron had a severe gash across his forehead. Everyone was dazed but, unbelievably, no one had major injuries.

We were confronted by several Germans with machine-pistols. I realized that the ground floor had given way beneath the AVRE, and we had fallen through into a cellar. I looked around and saw that holes had been knocked in the dividing walls between all the cellars of the terrace, creating a sort of dugout. We were shoved roughly through a gap into the next cellar, stripped of our valuables and made to sit with our backs to the wall. The room was lit by a couple of oil lanterns. Outside, the Canadian artillery opened fire. From all round came the sound of exploding shells. Plaster rained down from the ceiling.

'The Geneva Convention requires that as prisoners of war we must be taken to a place of safety,' said Ron.

'There is no place of safety,' snarled a big German sergeant-major. 'Your artillery and warships have seen to that. You'll have to take your chances with the rest of us!'

I was still feeling a bit stunned but I listened to the Germans talking among themselves. I didn't recognize their dialect and some of them lapsed into a language I did not understand. One of them, a medical orderly, came across to bandage Ron's head.

'You're not German, are you?' I said.

He shook his head.

'I am Polish, and so are many of my comrades,' he said. 'When Poland was conquered in 1939 we became prisoners of war. Later, we were offered the chance of fighting the Russians in the German Army or becoming slave workers. What would you have done? In the end, they sent us to France – you know what armies are like.'

'There are many Poles fighting Hitler in the British Army,' I said. 'When this battle is over, will you join them?'

'Perhaps,' he said.

'Stop talking to the prisoners!' barked the sergeant-major.

A few moments later a field telephone rang. The sergeant-major answered it.

'Battalion briefing – keep a good lookout,' he said shortly, then left the cellar.

'Listen,' I whispered to the others, 'I think we can talk them round. Just play along with whatever I say.'

Everyone nodded. No one had a better idea and they seemed to trust me.

'Anyone interested in football?' I said genially to our captors, then pointed to Jock. 'You're in luck – this is the Great McCabe, the famous Scottish international. I expect you've heard of him.'

Jock played in goal for the squadron team, although he wasn't very good. Whenever he did manage to stop the other side scoring he would give us a grin and shout something like, 'Another magnificent save from the Great McCabe!'

Our captors, obviously not wishing to be thought ignorant in football matters, seemed impressed.

'So, we are meeting the Great McCabe!' said one of them. 'How many times have you played for Scotland?'

Jock entered willingly into the spirit of the

thing. I translated the details of the remarkable career he described. He had apparently played for Rangers *and* Celtic in turn and taken part in notable Scottish victories over the USSR, Denmark, Liberia and Siam, to name but a few. The audience was interested and asked questions to which he supplied equally remarkable answers.

'Ask them if Hitler plays football,' said Gloomy.

I thought that while the Poles would probably be amused by the idea, some of the Germans might not, so I ignored Gloomy's suggestion. The conversation became relaxed and friendly. In the end we even began showing each other our family photos.

'You know, this is stupid,' I said eventually. 'In the morning, the attack will start again. You've seen the way things are going and there's just no point in any of us getting killed when we know how the battle is going to end. Why don't you let us take you over to our lines? You'll be decently treated and the war will be over in a few months, anyway.'

The Poles agreed eagerly, but some of the Germans were suspicious.

'How do we know this is not a trick?' asked one of them.

'Well, look at it this way,' I replied. 'What's the point in carrying on when those of you who survive will be prisoners in 24 hours? You'd better make your minds up quickly, before that sergeant-major of yours gets back.'

That seemed to do the trick. To my relief, and everyone else's surprise, they laid down their weapons and quietly followed us.

We scrambled over the rubble-covered wreck of *Invincible* and out into the fresh air. The shelling had stopped. As we approached our lines, we were challenged. Once our identity had been verified we were allowed to lead the prisoners forward in single file.

'I can't believe you got away with that,' muttered Gloomy, chuckling to himself.

The major commanding the Canadian infantry company, greatly amused by our escape, sent forward one of his platoons to occupy the position. I smiled to myself and wondered what the German sergeant-major would think when he returned from his battalion briefing!

Next morning the squadron's armoured recovery vehicle arrived. As *Invincible* was lying nose-down at an angle of 45 degrees, it took a strong pull from both the ARV and Mr Francis's AVRE to get her out. It involved several hours of hard work to get her started, and even then she coughed and spluttered.

'I'm afraid we'll have to leave you out of today's operations,' said Mr Francis. 'She's in no fit state to go into action.'

'I'm willing to have a go, sir, if the other lads agree,' I said. 'One of the Poles we brought in told me that there's a V-2 launching site in this copse, just beyond the enemy's next defence line.'

I pointed to the spot on the map. Mr Francis shook his head.

'I'm sorry, but I'm not prepared to take the chance. If you broke down you'd be a sitting duck.'

'It's personal, sir,' I said. 'You see, Gloomy and I live in the area where these things are landing – we'd like to sort this one out, for the sake of our families.'

Mr Francis was a good officer and I didn't want to add to his worries in action, but I wanted to be involved in this battle. After thinking hard for a minute he glanced at Ron, who nodded slightly.

'All right – against my better judgement,' said the troop leader. 'We cross the start-line at 1500 hours. You've got until then to get *Invincible* into some sort of order.'

*

We did what we could, but it took all my skill to keep her moving. The assault group included Crocodiles and infantry, and its task was to break through a line of concrete bunkers and pillboxes. In the event, the enemy didn't put up much of a fight and some of his positions were deserted. While the prisoners were being rounded up I spotted the copse the Pole had told me about, some 400 yards ahead. Ron had seen it, too.

'Off you go, John,' he said. 'This is your party!'

I had half expected the copse to be deserted as well, but as we approached I could see the silver nose-cone of a rocket protruding above the trees. The sight made me very angry. Smashing our way through the young trees, we entered a clearing. The rocket was standing vertically on its tail fins with some sort of vapour coming out of it. There were men fussing round it, going through the launching drill.

Gloomy's normally expressionless face was a mask of fury. He fired a long continuous burst straight into the rocket. The explosion was immense. A gigantic fireball filled the clearing, devouring everything in its path, including several

155

vehicles under camouflage nets. I felt its searing heat as it rushed towards the AVRE, washed over it and rolled back.

'You maniac!' shouted Ron as the smoke and flames cleared. 'Why didn't you warn me? You've burned my eyebrows off!'

As we left the copse, *Invincible*'s engine spluttered, died and refused to start again. Her part in the war was over, and for the moment so was ours. We hitched a lift on one of the infantry trucks and later that afternoon reached the coast. Across the Channel I could see the white cliffs of Dover, the first sight of home since I had sailed with the D-Day invasion fleet.

Over the next few days we helped out where we could. By 29 September the Pas-de-Calais area was firmly in Allied hands. For the first time since 1940 the Kent coast was free from enemy gunfire and, even more important, we had removed the threat of rocket attacks on London and south-eastern England. Our crew made a bonfire to celebrate.

'Well,' I said, spooning compo stew into my mouth, 'that's put an end to Herr Hitler's tricks.'

'Oh, I expect he'll have something else up his sleeve,' said Gloomy sadly.

Ron, darning a sock on the other side of the fire, threw his boot at him.

'I'll stick something up your sleeve if you go on like that!' he shouted and we all laughed – even Gloomy.

Chapter 15
Epilogue

Sadly, that was the last time we were all together before the war ended. After all her adventures, *Invincible* would require a complete refit and, for the moment, we were left with little to do. Ron went the next morning. The powers that be had decided that he had done more than his share of fighting and he was sent to one of the division's instructional wings.

Mike left a few days later to start his officer training. Next, George was posted to divisional headquarters, where they gave him a third stripe and made him adviser to the principal demolition officer. Jock was promoted but stayed with the squadron as Major Tunstall's signals NCO. Gloomy was finally rewarded with a stripe. I was glad because, for all his unusual ways, he was a useful and hard-working member of the crew. About a week after his promotion I was sent away on an AVRE commander's course. After that I was posted to another assault engineer regiment.

So there it was. The six of us had all come from very different backgrounds, shared an extremely violent period of our lives, then gone our separate ways again. We stayed in touch, however, and we never miss a reunion. Whatever we have become since, for a few hours once a year we are Ron, George, Mike, Jock, Gloomy and John again – six young soldiers who laugh at the same old jokes and some of the things that didn't seem quite so funny at the time. Our comradeship was born of shared hardships, danger, fear, understanding and, finally, success. It is something we value highly, and something that can never be taken away from us.

Normandy and After

On D-Day the 79th Armoured Division's breaching teams used 50 Crabs and 120 AVREs, of which 12 and 22 respectively were knocked out. Casualties among their crews amounted to a total of 169 killed, wounded and missing, which, given the nature of their task, was very low. By midnight on 6 June, 57,000 American and 75,000 British and Canadian troops had been put ashore. On the British sector alone, 950 fighting vehicles, 5000 wheeled vehicles, 240 field guns, 280 anti-tank guns and 4000 tons of stores had been landed.

Some had anticipated that the invasion would cost tens of thousands of casualties. On Gold, Juno and Sword Beaches, where the British and Canadians landed, losses amounted to just 4200 killed, wounded and missing. Apart from a few DD Shermans, the Americans had no specialist armour and sustained some 6000 casualties.

Major-General Hobart's division, the largest in any of the Allied armies, changed the face of war for ever. Its assault teams took every obstacle in their stride, whether they were man-made or natural defences. Its equipment covered the widest possible range of tactical requirements. Apart from the AVRE in its many forms and the explosive devices it used, the Crab, the DD Sherman and the terrible Crocodile flame-thrower, the divisional 'zoo' contained many more specialized armoured vehicles.

There was the Kangaroo, an armoured personnel carrier for the infantry, consisting either of a self-propelled howitzer with the weapon removed, or a turretless Sherman or Canadian Ram tank. There was the amphibious Buffalo, a tracked landing vehicle originally developed for the Pacific theatre of war, and its smaller cousin the Weasel. And finally there was the so-called Canal Defence Light (CDL), a Lee/Grant tank chassis and hull fitted with an immensely powerful light reflected through a narrow slit by the rapid movements of a mechanically driven shutter. The effects of this light could include temporary blindness, nausea and loss of balance. It also prevented the enemy identifying the source of the light. It was possible for troops to advance on a brilliantly illuminated objective, yet remain invisible in the inky blackness between two CDL beams.

After assisting in the capture of the Channel ports, the 79th Armoured Division was closely involved in clearing the enemy garrisons from South Beveland and Walcheren in the Scheldt estuary, so opening the great port of Antwerp for Allied supplies. In February 1945 it smashed the northern end of the Siegfried Line during the Reichswald battle, and subsequently took part in the Rhine crossings and the advance across Germany. In addition, its assault teams fought numerous minor battles in support of British, Canadian and American operations.

By the end of the war the divisional strength amounted to 21,430 men and 1566 armoured fighting vehicles (AFVs); the strength of a conventional armoured division was about 14,400 men and 350 AFVs. One of the most remarkable facts about the division's history was that both the nature of its equipment and the operations it undertook were concealed from the general public until after the Rhine crossings. The press then produced reports which fell just short of claiming magical powers for Major General Hobart, his men and their equipment.

The Significance of Hobo's Funnies

Prior to the formation of the 79th Armoured Division, the invasion of France by the Allies had seemed impossible. The use of specially designed armoured vehicles was crucial to the success of the Allied offensive action.

● By combining the principles of armoured warfare with assault engineering techniques, the 79th Armoured Division had rendered every aspect of the German defences useless.

● As a result of the division's success, the war in North-west Europe was brought to an end much sooner than if more conventional means had been employed.

● Most important of all, because of tactics and equipment developed by the division, countless Allied lives were saved.

Glossary

Aide-de-camp – the personal assistant to a general, usually identified by a set of ornamental shoulder cords.

AVRE – Assault Vehicle Royal Engineers

Ball race – a circle of ball bearings in a tank's hull that allows the turret to revolve on top of it.

Beachhead – the area occupied by an invasion force immediately after it has landed.

BESA – British Enfield Small Arms, the manufacturers of the machine-guns used by the AVRE.

Breaching team – a grouping of specialist armoured vehicles acting together to overcome various aspects of the enemy defences.

Brew up – slang name for making tea; also used to denote an armoured vehicle that has been set on fire.

Compo – slang name for Composite Rations.

Element C – a metal triangular structure fitted with explosives, used on beaches as a defence against attack.

Fascine – a large bundle of brushwood or other material that could be dropped into a ditch or crater to provide a way across.

Flying Dustbin – slang name for the blunt-nosed bomb fired from an AVRE's 290 mm petard; also called General Wade's Flying Dustbin.

LCT – landing-craft tank.

Net, wireless – several wireless sets working together on the same radio frequency.

Petard – a type of bomb-throwing spigot-mortar fitted to an AVRE.

Track horns – the foremost portion of the upper run of a tank's tracks.

FACTS AND FIGURES

● **NAVAL STATISTICS**

c200,000 men engaged in naval operations on D-day
(two thirds British)
c6,900 ships assembled for the invasion including:
7 battleships
2 15 in gun monitors
23 cruisers
2 gun boats
103 destroyers
221 escorts
287 minesweepers
4 minelayers
1 seaplane carrier
8 headquarters landing ships
anti-submarine escort groups
495 motor torpedo and motor gun boats
2 midget submarines (to be used as boundary markers)
4,126 different types of landing craft
736 ancillary vessels
10 hospital ships
59 blockships (to be sunk and act as part of the
breakwaters)

● **AIR STATISTICS**

c14,000 air sorties were flown on D-day
c3,700 allied fighters were airborne including:
15 squadrons covering shipping
54 squadrons giving beach cover
36 squadrons supporting ground operations
33 squadrons taking part in offensive operations
33 squadrons available for immediate deployment as
required

6,000 tons of bombs were dropped in the two hours
before the beach assault began.
8,000 British and 16,000 American airborne troops
landed by parachute and glider.

● **LAND STATISTICS**

Troops put ashore on D-day:
c75,000 British and Canadian
c57,000 US

● **CASUALTIES**

4,200 British and Canadian
6,000 US

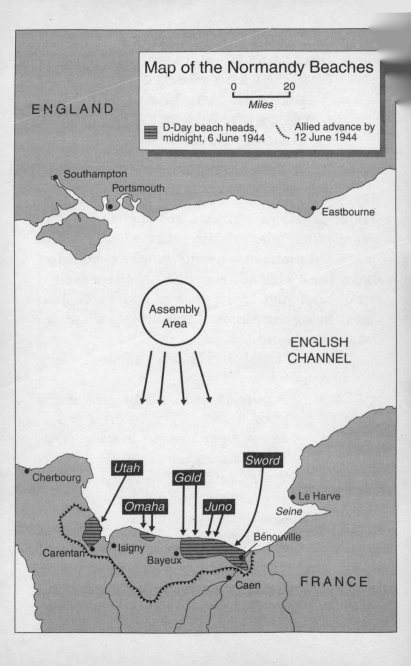

**What was it like to fly
a Lancaster plane during
the Second World War?
Find out in the next
Warpath adventure,
Night Bomber ...**

By now we were at 22,000 feet and flying at about 200 mph through the night sky. The noise from the Merlin engines filled the plane. Without our headphones we wouldn't have been able to hear one another, even if we'd been just a few inches apart. We had been flying for almost three hours when we finally saw land.

'German coast five miles ahead,' Wally warned.

'Roger,' responded Bob. 'Want to check your guns, fellas?'

'Roger that, skipper,' came Steve's voice through my headphones.

Steve fired first, letting off a burst to clear his guns of any ice that might have formed. When he'd finished, Bruce did the same.

Wally let us know that we were about to cross the German coast.

'Roger,' said Bob. 'OK, Andrew, throw out the Window.'

This 'Window' was a new device. The boffins had come up with it some time ago, but it was only in the last few weeks that Bomber Command had actually been allowed to use it. 'Window' was the name given to thin strips of tinfoil, each one a foot long by half an inch wide. They were packed into bundles, held together by brown paper. Andrew's job was to push these bundles down a chute. As soon as they hit the slipstream of the Lancaster, the paper burst open and the thin strips of tinfoil scattered and drifted towards the ground, completely disrupting enemy radar.

So far it had been a fairly quiet trip.

'Ten minutes to target,' Wally informed us.

'Fighter coming in from the rear!' Bruce suddenly shouted.

I heard the chatter-chatter-chatter of his gun. Steve's gun, in the middle upper position, joined in the action and I could also hear the whine of tracer from the incoming fighter.

We were in trouble.

'Coming in from starboard!' shouted Bruce.

Bob immediately turned the Lancaster to port to miss the line of tracer from the German fighter, and then swung the heavy bomber back again. He began to weave the huge plane from side to side, desperately trying to avoid enemy fire. From both outside the plane and coming through my headphones, the sound of gunfire was deafening.

Suddenly there was an explosion on our starboard side that lit up the night sky.

'Got him!' roared Steve.

'Five minutes to target,' reported Wally.

'Taking up position at the bombsight,' Andrew replied.

As we approached the target I could hear Andrew's voice guiding Bob towards it.

'Right . . . steady . . . right . . . steady . . . left . . . right a bit more . . . OK.'

We were over the target. There was a click as Andrew released the bombs.

'Bombs gone!'

We all waited for the plane's usual surge upwards as the bomb load left, making us that much lighter. But it didn't happen.

'What's up?' called Bob. 'Something wrong?'

'The mechanism's jammed!' Andrew shouted. 'The bombs are stuck in the bay!'